What's
Happily Ever After,
Anyway?

Brown Barn Books
Weston, Connecticut

What's Happily Ever After, Anyway?

Brown Barn Books
Weston, Connecticut

Brown Barn Books,
A division of Pictures of Record, Inc.
119 Kettle Creek Road, Weston, Connecticut 06883, U.S.A.
www.brownbarnbooks.com

Library of Congress Control Number: 2004105924
ISBN: 0-9746481-3-2

Taylor, Michelle.

WHAT'S HAPPILY EVER AFTER, ANYWAY? A novel by Michelle Taylor

Printed in the United States of America

For K.S.D.

oпe

My birthdays always consist of a few small gifts, chocolate cake, and off-key singing. For my sixteenth, I would've loved a new car or a raging party with a band and catered food. But for a family like mine, I knew I had a better chance of meeting up with my fairy godmother. I never in my wildest fantasies expected a gift that would carry me away from my ordinary existence forever.

My friend Tasha woke me up before seven o'clock on the first day of summer vacation with a shrill ring of the telephone. "Miranda?"

"Mmmmm," I mumbled. My morning voice is always husky, even though I've never smoked a cigarette in my life.

"Did I wake you up?"

"Nah, I had to answer the phone anyway." I kept my eyes closed. "What's up?"

"I just won four tickets to the concert tonight! I was the seventh caller. You know the morning show on the radio?" Actually, I didn't, but Tasha had three radio stations on speed dial.

I jumped up in bed, making a grab for my pale blue comforter as it slid to the floor. I missed. "Are you serious? Backstage passes?"

"I wish. Third-row center, though."

"Sweet. This is an invitation, right?"

"Well, duh. I had to get you something for your birthday."

"This covers Christmas, too. So awesome." I got up and pulled out my dresser drawer for some shorts.

Tasha said with a hint of laughter, "What about asking your brother?"

I shifted the phone into my other hand so I could struggle out of the jersey I wear to bed. "Tash."

"I'm just kidding. Lighten up. But, you know, that boy could use some fun in his life."

Mack is barely a year older than I am, and most of the time we get along okay, even though in public I like to pretend he doesn't exist. It makes me crazy that my friends think he's cute. I don't want to hear about how my brother has a nice ass.

Tasha changed the subject. "Will your parents let you go, it being your birthday and all?" She knows how much I hate my so-called wholesome family life. Roast beef dinners at six. Parents who have to know where I am and who I'm with at any given moment. Tasha never had to ask permission to do anything.

I rolled my eyes. "Of course they'll let me go. Who else is coming?"

"Carly and maybe her friend Tami." Carly was Tasha's older sister. "I'll call you later when I figure out who's driving."

Actually, I knew Mom and Dad weren't going to be thrilled about me going to a concert. It wasn't just the candles and the cake either. They lived through the seventies and knew all about what goes on in a crowd sailing on good music. Mom liked Tasha but thought Carly was kind of wild. She had a two-year-old son and she was only nineteen. On the other hand, it was my birthday, so I thought I'd take advantage it. And if they said no, I'd figure out a way to get there anyway.

Ali, my little sister, was in the kitchen making orange juice. Half of it was on the floor. "Hey, Ali-cat," I said. "Did Mom and Dad already go to work?"

She giggled and then Mom and Dad popped out of the pantry yelling "HAPPY BIRTHDAY!" I shook my head. They are so dumb sometimes for being such smart people.

"Guess what?" I said a few minutes later, when Mom had taken over the juicing and Dad was spongeing up the mess. "Tasha won tickets to the Rock Fest concert tonight."

"Rock Fest? Is that the concert where all those boy bands play?" Dad asked. I ignored him.

"Tasha invited me."

"What about the cake?" Ali wanted to know. She was only seven, young enough to still get excited about ancient traditions. She was now pouring Cheerios into a bowl.

I got the milk out of the refrigerator for her. "Well, we can have it early."

"I suppose we could," Mom hesitated. "But Miranda, I really don't…" She stopped and looked at Ali, who was spooning the cereal in her mouth as fast as she could. I tried not to laugh. Mack had told her that the faster she ate, the faster the vitamins started working. We both adored teasing her.

Taking advantage of the distraction, I cut in. "Come on, Mom, you just have to let me go. It's my birthday. It's not like I'm asking for a car."

She looked at Dad. He shrugged his shoulders. And that's how I managed to get a third-row-center ticket to the hottest concert of the summer. I had no idea that ticket was going to change my life.

I'd been to concerts before. The summer I was ten the whole family went to see Jimmy Buffet. Mack and I took Ali up to the grassy area of the outdoor amphitheater and played with her. She was just learning to walk then. We went back to our seats when the music started. Mom and Dad were swaying to the beat. When I was young I loved watching Mom's hair swish around her face as Dad spun her. I used to watch their feet. They'd laugh at me, but they'd slow down so I could learn their moves. Then we all went to see Joe Cocker when I was thirteen. He was really old and his voice sounded like he'd inhaled a million pounds of harsh chemicals. And I had reached the age when watching my parents dance in public was gross.

So Rock Fest marked my first concert without my family. But I didn't bother to share that with Tasha. She and her sister were seasoned fans. Carly had some body paint and she asked me to put a tiger on her shoulder blade. Drawing is my thing.

Tami whistled in admiration when I put the finishing touches on the tiger after only a few minutes. "Wow. That's awesome. How about a butterfly here?" she asked me, pointing to her bare upper arm. We'd never met before.

"Sure." I really didn't mind and I still had time to check out the crowd as we stood in line waiting to be frisked for glass containers and weapons. There were shirtless guys everywhere. Right before the gates opened, I pointed out a tall, dark guy with a scorpion tattooed on his arm. "There you go, Tasha."

Tami looked over my shoulder. "Oh yeah. He's hot." Carly waved and gave him a slow, sexy smile. He grinned and waved back.

Tasha glared at Carly. "That's just what you need in your life—a criminal."

"That's the best kind," I said, winking at Carly. She laughed, but Tasha rolled her eyes.

Tasha and I had been friends since seventh grade. We were locker neighbors, and the first day of junior high we had the same classes and were wearing the same bright orange nail polish. Even back then, Tasha was smart about boys. She appreciated the boring boys like my brother—the ones who did their work and never gave the teacher any trouble. I always liked the popular boys. The shallow boys, Tasha said. I had those drama-packed junior high relationships where you don't really go anywhere but hold hands between classes and write each other's names on your notebooks and profess undying devotion until you break up after two days or two weeks.

So I guess it was no big surprise in high school that I was the first one to get involved and the first one to lose my virginity. Not that I slept around or anything. It was one guy, Ryan, my freshman and sophomore years. Ryan was supposedly a good boy. He was on student council, played football, and always called my parents

"Ma'am" and "Sir." Sex started early in the relationship when I was still impressed with the status of being with such a "popular" guy. I did what I had to do to hang on to that. And Ryan made it fun, slipping a little rum into our Cokes and wearing glow-in-the-dark condoms. I figured as long as we were being safe, it was harmless. Passion could come later. We had our picture in the yearbooks as "Couple of the Year," all innocence and smiles. Tasha shook her head when she saw it and said I hadn't outgrown my shallow stage. After watching her sister make mistakes over guys, she considered herself sort of an expert. I thought I could take care of myself, so I didn't pay much attention when she tried to warn me about Ryan.

I knew I wasn't going to spend the rest of my life with Ryan, but I figured he was good practice until something better came along. The way I saw it, "something better" might be a hot boy at a wild rock concert.

I was into the music right away. Tami and Carly were too cool to dance. Tasha mostly just swayed her hips and sang along with the words. I was the one who really let go. I tossed my hair back and put all my moves together. The boys in the row in front of us were paying more attention to us than what was happening on the stage. They were all too cool to dance, though, except the boy farthest from me. He had the moves. And he was cute. He had on a shirt with cut-off sleeves and he hadn't buttoned it, so I could see his smooth, tan chest. The muscles in his arms were the kind you get from working outside—long and lean. He smiled when he caught me looking and danced his way past his buddies towards me. They all high-fived him or slapped his shoulder. Tami and Carly laughed and shouted, "All right, Miranda!"

Tasha gave me a warning look. "Behave yourself," she mouthed.

I pretended I didn't catch her words and leaned into the boy as he shouted into my ear, "I'm Keith!"

"Miranda!" I couldn't see his hair color in the darkness; it seemed light. He looked great in faded, loose, frayed jeans. I switched my rhythm a beat, so the movement of our hips matched. He smiled, and that's when I noticed his dimples. My dream guy always had dimples.

We danced through every song. I could feel the sweat on my forehead and gathered up my hair to cool off the back of my neck. Keith wiped sweat off his upper lip. He took a plastic cup from the guy next to him and handed it to me. Tasha had told me not to drink from anyone's cup. She had this thing about alcohol. I took a long drink. It was just Pepsi, icy and sweet. The first ballad started. Keith put his hand on my shoulder and leaned close to my ear. "I love this song. You want to dance?"

He put his hands on my bare skin where my tank top didn't meet the top of my jeans. I could feel calluses on his fingertips, but his touch was gentle and he didn't try to pull me tight against his body. I let my cheek brush lightly against his shoulder, taking in the smoothness of his skin. I wanted that song to go on forever.

After the show, he took my hand so we wouldn't get separated in the sea of sweaty bodies. We stopped at the exit gates and exchanged numbers, writing on our ticket stubs with my blue eyeliner.

The last thing he said was, "You're a great dancer, Miranda." He sort of blushed, then leaned over and kissed me on the cheek. "Later. I hope." And he was gone into the crowd. But I was just plain gone.

two

When I got home from the concert, I sank into the grass in the front yard, holding the ticket stub in my hands. The sky had a million stars and the cool night air was refreshing after hours of dancing, the long car ride, and Tami's cigarette smoke. The house was silent and dark, but I knew stepping inside would erase the magic of the night. I didn't want to go back to being ordinary Miranda Watson.

Mom was still awake, whispering a story to Ali in the glow of a night-light. The enchanted spell I was under made me forget for a minute that I was too cool for our little family rituals. I let down my guard a little and crept into Ali's room, entranced by the power of my mother's storytelling voice.

As I crouched in the shadows near Mom's feet, I remembered the tales she had made up especially for me when I was a little girl. Elaborate fairy tales with evil witches, castles in the sky, and princes on white horses coming to the rescue. Happily ever afters. That was always the best part—the happily ever after part. Mom sometimes would try to tell me other stories, but I'd demand princesses. Ali hated happily ever afters; her stories were about girls who went on adventures in the rain forest or about girls who wore combat boots.

After the story, Mom put her arm around me and we walked to my room at the end of the hall. "How was the concert?" she whispered.

"Great." I let one word sum it up. "How come you're still awake?"

"Ali and I stayed up watching movies because you and Mack were both gone. But I'm too old to be up this late." She stifled a yawn.

"I'm tired too, Mom."

"You can tell me about the concert in the morning."

I was glad to go straight into my room and tuck the ticket stub with Keith's handwriting into my mirror. I fell into bed to dream about Prince Keith and Princess Miranda.

I got my driver's license the next day, so discussing the concert was pushed back. Everyone acted like the license was a big deal. Dad took off from work to go with me to the testing center, and Ali gave me a grubby penny to put in my pocket for good luck. Mom even called from the office to give me last-minute tips on parallel parking.

I was probably the least excited, even though I should have been glad to live in Colorado, one of the few states left to grant driving privileges at sixteen. But it wasn't like I was getting my own car. I was going to share an old battered Jeep with Mack. Like he'd ever let me drive. In fact, I sort of wondered if there was a family conspiracy to keep me home. But Mack seemed pleased when I came home with the license in my back pocket.

He handed me a freshly copied key and said, "Welcome to the Watsons' Limousine Service. You will be the new escort of one Alison Watson to countless birthday parties, ballet lessons, and Brownie meetings. Buckle up and smile and don't expect a big tip."

He grabbed his basketball and headed out to the driveway. "By the way, Tasha called."

The phone rang before I got a chance to call her back.

"Hello!" Ali shouted, triumphant at getting to the phone first. "Just a minute." Disappointed that it wasn't one of her giggly friends, she handed me the phone. "It's a boy." She picked up the sidewalk chalk she had dropped in her mad dash to the phone and went outside.

"Hello," I said, taking the phone up to my room.

"Hi. This is Keith. From last night."

As if I had forgotten! "Hi. What's up?" I kept my voice relaxed, but pulled the ticket stub from the mirror. His handwriting was small and angular.

"Not much. Did you have fun last night?" His voice was deep and rich, something I hadn't picked up on before. I wondered if he sang.

"Yeah, I did. It was a great concert."

"Among other things," he said, and I couldn't help smiling. "So I thought I'd call and see if you wanted to do something sometime."

YES, I thought, but said, "I'd like that. So where do you live?"

"I live in the mountains west of Boulder. "

"Really? I live in Boulder. My mom works at the university."

"I live on a small horse ranch. Martin Farms. Have you seen the sign?"

I had seen the sign. "Small horse ranch" was an understatement. "How about you? Where do you live?" he asked.

"I live a couple of blocks from downtown. I go to Central High."

"Those girls you were with looked older. I was afraid you'd all be in college. What grade are you in?"

"I'll be a junior," I told him.

"I'll be a senior at Mountain View."

"Are you thinking about college?"

"My parents are thinking about college enough for me." He sounded resigned. "They want me to go to an agriculture program, but I don't know. They want me to run the ranch, but I can do that without going to school. I think I'd rather be a computer programmer or maybe an engineer. Or else maybe be a rock star."

I laughed. "My parents are engineers. My mom is a professor, but my dad owns a small construction company."

"I'd like that—owning my own business."

"Yeah, my mom helps with the blueprint stuff when she can. She likes computers, but my dad does most of the job site supervision. He's more the outdoor type."

"That's cool. My dad works with the horses and my mom is a music teacher."

"So what did she think about Rock Fest?"

"Well, she doesn't exactly call that stuff music."

We both laughed. Then he said, "So when would be good for you?"

"Well, I start lifeguarding at the pool next week. I don't know about my days off yet."

"How about this week, then—like tomorrow?'

That was soon, but I said, "Sure. What do you want to do?"

"How about Six Flags?"

"Yeah, that would be fun."

"One problem. I have a motorcycle. I could bring an extra helmet, but it would probably be better if I could drive over to your house and we get to the park another way."

Actually, I didn't even know if my parents would let me go to Six Flags with a guy I just met. I knew they'd say no to a motorcycle. Especially all the way to Denver. But I said, "I think that would be okay. I could use our car, or my brother, Mack, can drop us off."

"Your last name is Watson, right?"

"Yeah. Is my handwriting that bad?" I joked.

He laughed, "No, actually, I know a Mack Watson."

I couldn't believe this. This was unreal. Mack and I had a rule about dating each other's friends. "Are you sure?" I asked. "Watson isn't that unusual."

He went on. "Well, this guy plays in the All-City Baseball Summer League. I've been in two clinics with him. One last summer and one this spring. He plays center field. I mostly play left field, but we were partners in drills a couple of times. He goes to Central."

I sighed. Mack's life was baseball. "That would be my brother. Are you playing this summer?" I didn't have to rule him out yet. If he and Mack just played in a couple of clinics together, they couldn't have made friends. And they were opponents during the school year. All of a sudden I saw myself going to a lot of baseball games, which was sort of ironic since I've avoided them since back in Little League days.

"No, my dad hurt his shoulder breaking a horse, so I thought I'd hang out at home more this summer and help him on the ranch. I can play my senior year. Hey, maybe Mack would want to come to Six Flags with us?"

Tasha would fall on the floor when she heard this suggestion. Mack on my date. I closed my eyes for a second trying to picture it.

Keith noticed my hesitation. "I'm sorry. Of course you don't want your brother to come on our first date. That was a stupid thing to say."

Our first date. I could almost forgive him for the Mack thing. I laughed. "Well, maybe if he brought his own date."

"Only if he brings his own date," he agreed. "Do you know what time Six Flags opens?"

"I think ten. It's what, an hour's drive?"

"Okay—I'll be there around nine o'clock, then we won't have to wait in lines. At least not as much anyway. How do I get to your house?"

I gave him directions.

"Miranda," he said when I was finished, "I already know I'm going to have a great time."

I did too.

I immediately called Tasha. "Guess what? He called."

"Who? The boy from the concert?" She was nonchalant about it. "I knew he would. Cheek-kissers always call. So where is he taking you and when?"

"Six Flags. Tomorrow."

"We don't have much time then."

"Time?" I was confused.

"Yeah, to figure out what you're going to wear."

I laughed, "I thought I'd try clothes."

Tasha snorted, "There's so much you don't know."

I changed the subject, "Keith goes to Mountain View, and he knows Mack from baseball."

"You're kidding. This is like fate or something, Miranda. A guy who can dance and lives in the same city."

Tasha was teasing me, but for once I ignored it and continued with my summary. "He thought maybe Mack would like to double with us. What do you think?"

"Mack? On a double date? How are you going to pull that off?"

She was right about that. Mack may have been cute, but he was a lot more interested in baseball and getting straight A's than in his social life. "Well, you could go with him."

"I don't know, Miranda. Why don't you call one of those jock groupies that follow him around? They'd probably kill to get a chance to be with him."

Tasha was right. Giggly girls with shiny lip gloss and itty-bitty purses hanging off their arms were always swarming around Mack's locker. He was too polite to be rude to them, but he didn't seem much interested in them either. "Come on, Tasha, you know he won't want to spend a whole day with one of those losers. Help me out on this. Please."

"I'd go with him, but you always say your brother's off-limits."

"Okay, so I'll make an exception, for you. You can even talk about his ass."

Tasha laughed, "Okay, I'll go."

Tasha going with Mack to Six Flags was the perfect solution. Mom and Dad would think Tasha and I were going to catch some rays at the water park and Mack and his buddy were going to be macho on the roller coasters.

"That's one problem solved. I do have Ali to worry about. Mack and I are supposed to watch her this week. Her summer camp doesn't start till next week. Mom's busy getting ready for summer session. I refuse to take my seven-year-old sister on a date. Mack is bad enough."

"You should have a family like mine, and then you wouldn't have these problems." Tasha's mom worked at a makeup counter at a big department store in the mall and bartended a couple of nights a week at a place on Pearl Street. Her dad had been out of the picture for a long time. I never knew what to say when she made jokes about her family. Tasha didn't seem to notice. "Well, if you can't think of anything, she can hang out with Carly. I've watched Josiah enough lately. Let me know, so I can tell her."

Mack was still shooting hoops in the driveway. Ali was writing her name on the sidewalk with chalk. I sat down in the grass next to her and called to Mack, "Hey, do you know Keith Martin from the All-City League?"

He missed a free throw. "Yeah—we had a clinic together last spring. He plays center field for Mountain View."

"I met him at the concert last night. What's he like?"

Mack rebounded a layup and flopped, sweating, on the grass next to me. "I don't know, Miranda. It's not like I take notes on guys my sister might be interested in, but I don't think he's your type. He seems like a decent guy." That was a dig about Ryan—Mack hated him. "He's a good ballplayer, fast and a magician with the bat. I think he has horses or lives out in the country or something. He had cowboy boots in his locker." Mack gave me a teasing look. "Never took you for a cowgirl."

I glared at him. "Well, he didn't have boots on at the concert, and he wants to take me to Six Flags tomorrow."

Mack raised his eyebrows. "Are you going?"

"I told him I would. But I guess I need to run it by Mom and Dad. He doesn't have a car, only a motorcycle."

"I wouldn't mention the motorcycle on the first date."

"That's what I thought. Keith thought maybe I could drive."

Mack laughed. "Did you tell him you just got your license today?"

"What do you think? I told him I could probably drive or you could drop us off. But guess what? He remembered you and thought maybe you'd like to come."

Mack laughed, "That was smooth. I bet you loved that suggestion."

"Well, at first I didn't think it was so cool. But if you bring a date, I'd be okay with it." He stood up and dribbled the ball a few times before shooting another free throw, this time sinking it without touching the rim. He looked at me, shading his eyes from the sun. "I could ask Serena, that girl who calls all the time, but she's so boring."

"Tasha said she'd go with you," I coaxed, not quite believing I was offering that.

He plucked some grass and sprinkled it on Ali's head. She giggled and moved out of his reach. "And what about Squirt? Are you planning on leaving her home alone?"

I looked over at Ali. She had gotten bored with writing her name and was trying to make a butterfly. Her brown hair looked auburn in the sun. Mack and I have brown hair too, but ours is a lot lighter, especially in the summer, when it gets sun-streaked almost blonde. She was ignoring us, but I knew she was hanging on every word. "That's a thought," I drawled. "What do you think about spending the day all on your own, Ali-cat?"

She looked up. Blue chalk was smeared across her forehead and cheek. "I could go to Six Flags, too."

I glanced at Mack, looking for some help.

"How about you let Miranda and me go this time, and we'll take you to Six Flags and Waterworld later on this summer?"

I could tell Ali was torn. Should she whine and beg to go with us to Six Flags tomorrow, or take the bribe? "Well," she finally said. "My friend Megan invited me over to her house to go swimming this week. Mom said I could. I just don't know what day. Maybe I could go tomorrow."

Mack and I looked at each other. "That would be really cool, Ali," I said. "Do you think you could call Megan now?"

"If you make me some big butterflies and flowers to color."

"Sure." I picked up a piece of chalk and started drawing an outline for a giant garden on the driveway. Ali was gone about ten minutes. "Okay. And I called Mom too."

"You didn't tell her about Six Flags, did you?" I almost shrieked.

She put her hands on her hips. "What do you think? I'm not a dumb little kid anymore. You guys owe me big, so I want a present—one of those giant stuffed animals from the games."

"How did I get such bossy, sassy sisters?" Mack asked, turning Ali upside down and tickling her until I rescued her.

three

Mack made dinner that night—spaghetti, salad, buttery garlic bread. I sat at the counter and chopped vegetables. Normally I avoid the kitchen. In fact, cooking is considered a guy thing in our family. Mom can pour cereal and is a magician with eggs, but that's about it. Ali was starting to show an interest in cooking, too. So much for division of labor.

"So what do you think Mom and Dad will say about Six Flags?" I asked Mack.

"Probably not much if you're cool about it." He took the salad bowl from me, covered it, and stuck it in the refrigerator. He sat down at the counter across from me. "What's the deal with this guy, Miranda? You just met him."

I shrugged and took a sip of my ice water. Truth was, I had no clue why I was so excited about it all. I was never that way. Not about Ryan. Or actors. Or singers. Or anything for that matter; it wasn't my style. Even now I can't explain what made me feel the way I felt about Keith. But I didn't have to answer because just then, Dad came in from the garage.

"Yum," he said, going straight to the stove and lifting the lid on the simmering sauce. "My favorite. And you didn't even cheat."

When Mom made spaghetti she just warmed up sauce from a jar and added some mushrooms and Italian sausage. I liked that just as much as the homemade kind, but Dad and Mack thought it was some kind of crime against Italian cuisine.

"Where's Mom?" I asked.

"She wanted to work out for a while. I told her that you could go pick her up since you're our new chauffeur."

Mack turned down the heat on the sauce. "Should we wait for her?"

"She said to go ahead." Ali came in and jumped up on him.

"Did you see my picture in the driveway? Miranda made the outline for me, but I colored it all day." She had chalk dust smeared all over her knees and elbows in addition to her hands and face.

"Sure did. I even parked on the street so your Mom could see it."

Ali beamed, but I couldn't help rolling my eyes. Dad and Mom thought that art was a waste of my intelligence but would acknowledge any little scribble Ali made because she was the baby. Mack caught my expression and shrugged; we both agreed that Dad spoiled Ali to death. Oblivious to our reactions, Dad said, "Come on, van Gogh, let's go wash up. It's dinnertime."

"Mom tells me you're going swimming tomorrow," Dad said to Ali when they came back into the kitchen. We don't set the table. Usually we just serve ourselves from the stove then pull up a stool around the counter.

"My friend Megan has a pool."

"A real pool?"

"No, just one of those stand-up kinds from the toy store. We should get one."

I cut in, "I lifeguard at the pool all summer, silly. You can come anytime for free."

Dad turned his attention to Mack. "Do you know when you start this summer?"

Mack nodded. "Yeah, Tom called today. I start next Monday." This was Mack's second summer working with the community center's recreation program. The pay was lousy, but it was hard for him to find a job because he had baseball practice every day and games on the weekend. "So Miranda and I were thinking that since we both start working next week, and Ali's going to be at her friend's, we'd go to Six Flags tomorrow."

I almost choked on my salad. I thought the Six Flags trip would be all my deal.

Dad wiped spaghetti sauce off his chin and took a sip of water. "You two are going somewhere fun together? On purpose?"

I laughed. "We're going with other people too. It's not like we're going together."

"Yeah, this guy I know from baseball camp came up with the idea."

"Who's driving?"

"Mack," I said.

Dad waved his fork at Mack. "Make sure you let Miranda drive once in a while. She needs to drive on the interstate more."

I jumped in again, "I'd just rather not drive through the city with a whole bunch of people yet."

Mack grinned at me. I kicked him under the table.

Dad nodded. "Mom and I have an early meeting, so you'll have to drop Ali off at her friend's."

"No problem," Mack and I said together.

"Mack really is cool," Tasha said later when I told her about our dinner conversation.

We were in my room looking through my closet. Tasha had also brought over a shopping bag of stuff she called "amusement wear"—mostly tank tops and skimpy T-shirts from Carly's pre-baby days. I was all about skimpy clothes, but I'd have to leave the house looking like I was planning on hanging out with my brother and some friends. Six Flags had some wet rides and a small water park. I planned on wearing a new, royal blue bikini and was looking for something to put on over it. "Yeah, my brother's cool, when he wants to be, but I'll have to pay him back."

"That's for sure," Mack said, popping his head in the door. "Tasha, you want to go ride some roller coasters and help me chaperone my wild little sister?"

Tasha grinned at him. "It's a two-person job."

"Okay then. See you later." He shut the door.

There was a knock on the door and I said, "Now what?" expecting Mack again. It was Mom. She had showered and was in her robe with her wet hair brushed over one shoulder.

"Hey girls." She sat down next to Tasha's clothes piled on my bed. "Are you going to Six Flags too, Tasha?"

Tasha glanced at me. "Of course."

Mom looked at me, sizing me up. I didn't think she'd buy the baseball camp friend as easily as Dad did. I took out a pair of white overall shorts for something to do.

"Those will get too dirty," Mom said. Tasha nodded in agreement. I hung them back up.

Tasha sat with Mom on the bed and started shoving her stuff back in the bag. "I probably need to get home."

"You don't need to go, Tasha," Mom told her, picking up one of the shirts to help fold. The shirt was almost sheer and the kind of thing I was definitely not allowed to wear. "Miranda? Why do I feel like I'm not getting the whole story on this Six Flags trip? Who exactly is this boy?"

I glanced over at Tasha. She kept right on folding her clothes. "What boy, Mom? No one said anything about any boy."

"Miranda," Mom said.

"You might as well tell her," Tasha told me. She put the bag on the floor and leaned up against the wall.

"Oh. All right." I sat down on the floor, cross-legged. Mom stayed where she was, but settled against the pillows. "I met this guy Mack knows from baseball camp at the concert last night."

"Does he have a name?"

"Keith. Keith Martin."

"So this Keith person recognized you as a sister of a guy he knew for a week last summer?"

"No," I surrendered. "We were sitting near each other at the concert. We talked and exchanged phone numbers. Knowing Mack was just a weird coincidence."

Mom looked over at Tasha. "What do you think?"

"He's harmless," Tasha offered. "He kissed her on the cheek and invited her big brother on their first date. Not exactly what I'd call a lady-killer."

I glared at Tasha and then Mom laughed." Well, is he cute?"

"Mom," I said, exasperated.

Tasha laughed. "He's not bad."

"I'm so glad you two are having such a great time," I said, but I couldn't help smiling. There wasn't anything that could've spoiled my mood then.

I was ready at seven o'clock the next morning. Mom and Dad were down in the kitchen reading the paper. Ready for work, but waiting for coffee. "I thought you weren't leaving until nine," Dad said.

I poured some orange juice. "I couldn't sleep."

Mom put down the section she was reading and looked me over. "Why don't you French braid your hair? Then it won't get messed up if you get wet." Mom rarely commented on how my hair looked.

"Would you do it for me?"

She nodded, "Let's go up to my room." Mom hadn't braided my hair since Ali was born. Not because she didn't want to; I just wouldn't let her. I watched her in the mirror. I forgot how easy her touch was as her hands moved quickly through my damp hair. "Do you miss Ryan?"

I shrugged my shoulders. "Not really."

Her eyes met mine in the mirror for a second before she looked down at my hair. "I never really liked him."

"Really?" I was surprised. She never said anything like that before.

"Really. He was too polite."

I laughed. "He wasn't that polite all the time."

"I know—that's why I didn't like him." Her eyes met mine again, and for a moment I wondered how much she knew. I'd been really careful to not leave any clues. I kept condoms in my locker at

21

school; I never let Ryan leave hickeys where anyone could see them; and I was always home when I was supposed to be.

"Tasha didn't like him either, did she?"

"No."

"Why not?" She smoothed my hair between her fingers.

Mom watched me in the mirror. I could have told her that Tasha thought Ryan was using me; she didn't see how it could be a two-way street. But that was more information than I was willing to hand out.

I watched Mom bite her lip, thinking about something difficult. She met my eyes in the mirror. "Maybe it was…"

Her voice broke off. Dad came into the mirror carrying Ali on his back. He whistled at my reflection. Mom and I sort of smiled at each other, but I really wanted to know what she was going to say. What exactly did she know? I watched her go back to biting her lip. We had the same pale blue eyes. Everyone said she and I looked exactly alike. I always took that as a compliment because she is stunning.

Ali held out her arms to Mom. "Braid my hair, too."

Mom was still touching my hair, messing with the ends. She kissed Ali's cheek. "Get dressed first."

Ali wriggled from Dad's arms and raced across the hall.

Dad leaned against the bathroom counter facing Mom and me. "You know what, Miranda? Your mother and I went to a concert on our first date."

"Really?" I glanced at Mom. "I thought you guys met at a chemistry lecture."

"We did. She sat in the row in front of me, and she kept turning around to ask me for answers on the test."

"You wish," Mom said, sounding just like me. "I turned around all the time because he kept dropping his pencil, and I'd have to turn around and give to him. You were so obvious, honey."

Dad laughed, "Well, you must not have minded too much because you sure did say yes in a hurry when I asked you if you wanted to see Heart."

"Let me guess. One of those hard-rock seventies bands?" I joked, but kept my eyes on Mom. She was smiling, but her eyes were not.

Dad raised his eyebrows, "I think I probably have an album or two in the garage. You should listen to them."

"What's an album?" I teased, keeping my voice light. "Hey, Dad, did Mom kiss you on the first date?"

Dad looked at Mom. She leaned over and gave him a quick kiss on the cheek. "About like that," he answered, winking at me.

I leaned back against Mom and tilted my head up to see her face. "You guys are so boring."

They both laughed.

Dad walked to the door. "I need to get going. You want to ride together, Kate?"

Mom nodded. "Give me five minutes. Can you braid Ali's hair, Miranda?"

"Sure." I looked at myself in the mirror. "It looks great, Mom. Thanks."

She put her chin on my head. "Boring isn't so bad, baby girl."

Yeah, right. I thought to myself. She looked at her watch, then back at me. "Miranda?"

"What?" I met her eyes.

"Be careful." She kissed me on the cheek.

Keith was right on time. From the window, I watched him take off his helmet and comb his white-blonde hair with his fingers. He looked different in the sunlight. Better. Deeply tanned. Clean. Sexy. Ali watched next to me. "He's hot."

I looked down at her. "Where do you get that stuff from?"

She giggled and started to race to the door as the bell rang. I grabbed her arm. "I don't think so. Go get your towel."

I opened the door. "Hey."

His dimples just about killed me.

four

I would have invited Keith in, but Mack pulled the Jeep into the driveway before I had a chance. He'd gone to get gas so we wouldn't have to waste time on the way to Six Flags. I shook my head at him as he came to the doorway. "You're in for it now," I said.

Mack looked puzzled.

"Ali's garden," I reminded him, pointing toward the driveway.

"Oh, shit. Maybe she won't notice."

"Don't count on it."

Mack grinned at Keith. "Hey, man, how's it going?"

"Not bad. Thanks for driving."

"No problem." Mack looked at me. "I'll get Ali."

Keith and I started out to the Jeep. He had on faded loose Levi's again, and a green T-shirt. The T-shirt fit him tight. He smelled like cinnamon. "Who's Ali?"

"She's our little sister. We have to drop her off at her friend's."

We stood on the grass next to the driveway. It was hot already.

"Do you want to go to the water park?" he asked.

I pulled my T-shirt off my shoulder so he could see my bikini strap.

His smile was great, spreading slowly across his face, lighting up his eyes.

Ali and Mack came out then. Ali took one look at the smeared driveway and burst into tears. I didn't look at Keith to see what his reaction was but watched Mack pick her up. "Hey Ali-cat, I'm sorry. I was in a hurry and forgot." He was gentle with her, but she struggled to get free, so he let her go. She ran to me throwing her arms around my waist, burying her face against me. Great, I thought. Snot on the shirt I spent hours picking out. I pried her away from me and knelt down to look into her eyes. "You know, Ali, this is kind of a good thing."

"How?" She glanced sideways at Keith and realized she was throwing a fit in front of a stranger and tried to hide her face on my shoulder.

"Well, now that it's messed up, tonight, when you get home, you can get the hose and spray it all off. And I'll draw you a new picture. Won't that be fun?"

She sniffed. "Dad doesn't let me play with the hose. And besides, that coloring took me all day."

"I bet Dad will let you use the hose if I help you," Mack said. I winked at him.

Ali pulled her head away from my shoulder and looked at Mack. "Will you help me color a new picture if Miranda draws it for us?"

"Of course. I'm really sorry, Ali."

"Well, okay," she sniffed, drying off her face on her towel. She went over to the Jeep, keeping her eyes on the ground.

Keith nodded at Mack, "Is that your date, man?"

Mack laughed. "Sisters."

"Hey, now," I said.

Mack smiled at me. "I forgot my wallet. I'll be right back."

"He's a senior this year, right?" Keith asked when Mack had gone.

I shook my head. "No, we're both juniors."

He looked confused. "Are you guys twins?" It's a question we get asked a lot. Partly because we're in the same grade. Partly because we look so much alike. And lots of times we just say yes. It's easier than explaining the age difference. "No, we're ten months apart. He was born on August seventh and I was born the next year in June."

"June what?"

"June first."

He grinned. "You mean I met you on your birthday?"

I smiled back. His dimples just got better and better. "When's your birthday?"

"May eleventh. I can't believe you guys are only ten months apart. Your parents were crazy to have kids so close together like that."

"According to them, it was the plan. They said they wanted us to play together when we were little and double-date when we were older."

Keith laughed. "How old is Ali?"

"She's seven, going on three." Ali was peering under the Jeep, pretending to examine the streaks of her drawing. I knew she was listening, though. She always did.

"So you and Mack are built-in baby-sitters."

I nodded. "And she's a built-in chaperone."

Ali finally spoke up. "What's a chaperone?"

"Someone who asks lots of questions," I told her. She seemed satisfied with that answer. Keith and I traded smiles.

Our Jeep is a hand-me-down from Dad. An old battered white Wrangler with a soft top. In the summer, we take off the plastic and let the hot air blow around us. It's fun, but it cuts down on conversation. Ali climbed into the back, where we always made her sit.

"Hey, Ali," I said, "Why don't you sit up front this time?"

She gave me a puzzled look, but it was too big a treat for her to question it.

Mack winked at me. "That was sly."

"Shut up."

Keith just laughed.

We picked up Tasha after dropping Ali off. Mack cut the engine and leaped out to open the door for her.

"Oh Mack, thank you." She gave him a loud kiss on the cheek. They cracked up laughing.

Keith looked at me and raised his eyebrows. I shrugged like I didn't know what had gotten into them either.

We were about ten minutes early, and the ticket line was still short. Keith took his wallet out of his pocket and said to Mack, "I've got this covered."

Mack said, "Pay for Miranda. I'll take care of Tasha and myself." Tasha did a double take, but she didn't object. Money wasn't exactly flowing in her direction.

"Hey," I protested. "It's expensive. I'll pay for myself."

Keith touched my arm. "Let me pay. You can get lunch."

After deciding where to meet up later, Mack and Tasha walked off toward the roller coasters, and Keith and I were alone. "Let's get wet," he said.

Even though I walk around in my bathing suit all day long when I'm lifeguarding, I felt weird about being practically naked in front of a guy I really liked. I think Keith was kind of shy about it, too; he looked away when I slid off my shorts. I folded them carefully while he took off his jeans and busied myself with putting them in the locker we rented. I did slide him a look when he took off his T-shirt, noticing right away the Oriental symbols tattooed on his left shoulder blade. I wondered what they meant but didn't want to call attention to the fact that I was checking out his body.

"How about the pirate ship first?" he asked, turning to face me.

"Sure." The pirate ship was mostly for little kids—one big spraying, sprinkling, drenching jungle gym. I played on it with Ali, but Tasha and I always headed straight for the slides. Keith and I splashed through the ankle-deep water, climbed up onto a platform, ducked through a waterfall, and slid down a twisty slide. I went first, and Keith came so quickly after me that we both fell in the shallow pool. A little boy sailed out and landed across both of us. "Maybe we should try something our own size," I suggested when we untangled ourselves and finally stopped laughing.

We went on all the slides, until the lines got too long as people came in from other parts of the park to cool off. We ate pizza and rubbed sunscreen on each other's backs. He did my shoulders first, then quickly smoothed some lotion on the rest of my back. He blushed a little when he handed the bottle to me.

I took my time rubbing the lotion into his skin. His skin felt great, smooth and warm. I rubbed the lotion over the tattoo, noticing that the ink was jet black and not the dark green of home-made jobs. The lines were crisp and clean. "What does this mean?" I asked, tracing the first character with my finger.

"Harmony," he said, reaching around and touching my hand with his.

I smiled, liking that a lot.

The best part of the day was the wave pool. We rented a double inner-tube raft and paddled way out to the deep end to wait for the big ones. When we weren't getting swept in the current, we floated and talked. "Life doesn't get much better than this," Keith said at one point.

I smiled. "I love the water. Have you been to the ocean?"

"Once in Mexico. Once in Texas. Have you?"

"Yeah. We go somewhere with a beach almost every summer. My dad loves deep-sea fishing."

"My dad loves skiing, so we always take our vacations in the winter," Keith said.

"Do you have brothers or sisters?"

"A sister. Her name is Jody. She's in college."

"What's she majoring in?"

"Music. Do you play an instrument?"

I shook my head. "The guitar would be cool."

He nodded. "That's my favorite, but my mom made me learn what she considers more serious instruments."

"Like what?"

"Piano. Violin. Stuff like that."

"Are you in the band at school?" Tasha would never let me live it down if he was a band geek.

He splashed me. "I don't think so."

I splashed him back. "Well, I thought you could be one of those sexy drummer boys."

He laughed. "Nice save. Are you in sports?"

"I've been on the varsity swim team since freshman year."

"That's why you look so good in a bikini." His foot touched mine underwater. I blushed. I didn't think he'd noticed.

"Do you miss playing baseball this summer?" I asked, in a hurry to change the subject.

He nodded. "Yeah, but my dad needs me. He got thrown by a horse and stepped on a couple of times. It's taken a long time for his shoulder to heal. And we're training our horses, plus breaking five or six from other places. We also have cattle, so that's extra. I don't mind helping with the horses, and the cattle just graze in the summer. It's not too tough. Do you ride?"

"I have, but not a lot though. I like it. I like horses." Truth was, I'd ridden three times, and two of those times were ponies at a petting zoo when I was about four.

"Maybe you could come over sometime and we could take a ride. Have a picnic."

"Maybe," I said. But I couldn't think of anything more exciting. Or romantic.

I hated turning in our raft late that afternoon. Entering the crowded, noisy part of the park was like leaving a fairy tale. We held hands as we walked toward the exit to meet Tasha and Mack. They were already there with a big stuffed Sylvester cat and two medium-sized Tweety Birds. "Whoa," Keith said. "How much did that set you back?"

"You don't want to know," Mack said.

We drove back home with Sylvester belted in next to me, the Tweety Birds jammed in the space behind the backseat. We got some honks and waves on the interstate, but I didn't mind because Sylvester took more than his share of the seat and I had to sit in the middle with my thigh brushing up against Keith's. He draped his arm on the back of the seat, his hand casually on my shoulder. Life didn't get much better than that.

five

When we got home, Ali's drawings had been sprayed off, so Mack pulled in and parked next to Dad's truck. "I guess Ali talked Dad into letting her use the hose," Mack noted, leaping out of the Jeep and coming around to my side to wrestle the huge Sylvester out. He had left the Tweeties with Tasha when we dropped her off.

Keith took his arm from around me and gave the stuffed animal a shove toward Mack. "Thanks," Mack told him. "I'm going to be late for practice if I don't hurry."

"You want to come in for a while?" I asked Keith. I wasn't ready to say good-bye.

Keith hesitated. "Will your parents mind?"

"No, I don't think so. Besides, they probably want to meet you."

"And I should introduce myself. Anything I should be warned about? Is your dad one of those scary fathers who asks a lot of dumb questions?"

I laughed. "I don't think so. He'll probably ask if you want to stay for dinner."

The house was quiet, but I could hear Mom's voice on the deck. Lots of summer evenings Dad barbecues. Keith seemed a little nervous. He tucked his T-shirt into his jeans. I touched his arm. "Don't worry."

"Okay." He took my hand, and followed me through the kitchen. We both let go once we stepped outside. Dad was grilling hamburgers and Mom was stretched out on a deck chair, sipping a glass of wine.

"Hey, Miranda," she said. "Did you guys have fun?"

"Yep. This is Keith."

Dad reached out to shake his hand, and Mom waved from where she was.

"Where's Mack?" Mom asked.

"Getting ready for practice."

"That reminds me, his coach called. Practice is canceled for tonight. Would you tell him, Miranda?"

"Would you like to stay for dinner, Keith?" Dad asked, turning back to the burgers.

Keith looked at me for an answer.

"My dad is a magician on the grill," I coaxed. I didn't want him to leave even if we had to eat dinner with my parents.

Keith smiled. "I'd love to, but I need to call my parents first."

"Come on, I'll show you where the phone is." I left him in the kitchen and went to find Mack. I glanced into Ali's room. She was lying across her bed still in her bathing suit, asleep. Mack had put Sylvester on the bed next to her. She'd see him when she woke up. Mack rushed out of his room with his glove.

"Mom said that your coach canceled practice."

"No kidding?"

"That's what she said. She's on the deck. Dad's grilling."

"Sweet. Did Keith leave?"

"No, he's using the phone. Tell him I'll be down in a minute."

In my mirror, I noticed that my braids were all wispy and loose. I had gotten a little burned across my cheeks. I pulled my T-shirt off one of my shoulders; it was really stinging from the sun. I wanted to take a shower, but instead I went into my bathroom to take out my braids. I was almost finished when I heard a knock. Keith smiled from the doorway of my bedroom. "Mack told me to come up." He looked around the room, but stayed in the hall.

"You can come in," I told him, turning the light off in the bathroom.

He stayed where he was but leaned against the doorframe. "I don't want to get in trouble my first time here." His eyes sparkled when he smiled. "Wow. Did you paint this?"

I had turned my walls into a sky fantasy land by painting a castle surrounded by clouds and flowers and blue swirls. The furniture was plain. I had bunk beds that had originally been Mack's, but Tasha was always spending the night so we had switched. I had the beds set up in an "L" shape in the corner, so we could whisper all night. The comforters were pale blue with sunshine-yellow moons, and the floor was hardwood with star-shaped rugs.

"Yeah. Do you like it?"

"It's cool." I saw his eyes stray to the mirror over my dresser. Tucked under the edge of the frame were pictures of Mack, Tasha, Ali, and my old boyfriend, Ryan, along with birthday cards and the concert stub with Keith's number written on it. I didn't want Keith to see Ryan's picture and ask about it, so I went over and put one hand on his waist. It was the closest we'd been since slow-dancing at the concert.

"So I take it you have a guy room with trophies and baseball gloves and dirty socks on the floor?" I said.

"Something like that." He smiled at me and then touched my cheek with his fingertips. "You're burned."

"So are you." I put my other hand on the side of his face.

"Are you sure this is a good idea?" he whispered.

I didn't answer but moved my hand to his hair. It was rough from the wind and water. Our lips touched for a second, just as Mack yelled, "Dinner!"

Keith jumped back.

I rolled my eyes. "Great timing."

"I knew that was going to happen," Keith said, his voice still low. He took my hand, and this time, we didn't let go when we went outside.

The deck is my favorite part of our house. It runs the length of the south side of the house and has benches around the sides and a big picnic table at one end under the shade of a giant oak tree. In the fall we have to constantly sweep leaves, but in the summer the branches make the deck cool and relaxing. On the other end of the deck there are stairs leading to the yard. The sun always seems to hit that part no matter whatever time of day it is. Every year Mom and Dad talk about putting in a hot tub there but always decide against it. Dad says it would be too expensive; Mom says it would be too much work. Mack and I both think it would be awesome to have friends over to hang out in a hot tub. Mom always says, "Too much fun," when we try to convince her that the hot tub would be a good idea. I suddenly daydreamed of soaking with Keith in the moonlight and realized what she meant by "too much fun."

"Hurry up," Mack urged, breaking into my little fantasy.

"This is great," Keith said, biting into his burger. Dad beamed at him. He adores compliments on his cooking.

"Try the chicken," Mack mumbled, chomping into a drumstick. He grinned at us, barbecue sauce dripping from his chin.

Keith tried not to laugh. Mom thrust some napkins across the table toward Mack. "That's disgusting," she said, looking over at Dad for back-up. He was trying to get barbecue sauce off his shirt. Keith couldn't hold back his laughter, and Mack, Dad, and I joined him. Mom grinned too. "So much for table manners in front of company." She licked barbecue sauce from her fingers.

"So," Dad asked, "how was Six Flags?"

Mack answered, "Hot, but the lines weren't too long."

"I thought you were going to spend the day in the water park section?" Mom asked.

"Miranda and I did," Keith said, helping himself to another burger.

Mack added, "I wanted to, but we had to spend most of the time winning Ali that stupid stuffed animal."

Dad laughed. "Yeah, I heard all about how you destroyed the driveway art. I am afraid you'll have to help her restore the masterpiece tomorrow."

"Miranda is going to help," Mack said, pointing a fork at me.

I took a sip of my ice water. "Okay. You're lucky I don't have to go to the pool tomorrow."

"What do you do at the pool?" Keith asked.

Mack answered, "She works on her tan."

I kicked him under the table but said, "Yeah, basically. The life-guards rotate areas, but it's usually pretty boring. I give swimming lessons in the mornings to little kids."

"My dad keeps thinking we should have a summer riding clinic for kids."

Mom looked interested. "That's a pretty good idea actually. Ali would love something like that."

Keith grinned at her. "Well, don't tell my dad that. I have enough to do."

Ryan never joked with my parents. I could tell Mom liked Keith by the smile she flashed back at him.

"Your parents are cool," Keith said later when I walked him out to his motorcycle.

We stopped at the curb. I crossed my arms, feeling chilled despite the heat of my sunburn. The night air was cool after the heat of the sunshine. "They're okay."

"Are you cold?" Keith put his hand on my waist, drawing me close.

I shook my head. I wasn't cold standing near him like that. He smelled like chlorine and mesquite. "I had a great time today," I said, tilting my head back to look into his eyes.

"Me too." His voice was low again like it was in the doorway of my bedroom. I met his kiss. This time there were no interruptions.

As he drove off, I thought about what it would be like to ride off with him. It reminded me of every happily ever after ending in Mom's stories.

SIX

I don't know if it was from the sun, or the water, or if it was just because my first date with Keith was better than any fairy tale my mother had ever whispered to me, but that night I instantly fell into a deep and dreamless sleep. Ali slid her cold feet against my shins at first light, and I almost wished I had a dog instead of a little sister. I tried to pretend that I was still sleeping until I felt fur tickling my neck. She'd dragged the giant Sylvester into my bed. His arm flopped across me.

Mumbling, I asked, "What are you doing in here, Ali?"

"Couldn't sleep. I love my prize. Thanks."

"Thank Mack. He's the one who got it for you. Why don't you go tell him now?"

"I tried, and he threw his pillow at me."

Mack always was the smart one in the family. I shoved Sylvester's arm away and scooted closer to the wall. But it was no use; I was awake. I opened my eyes and looked over Sylvester at Ali. She grinned. It was impossible to be mad at her for long. No wonder she's so spoiled.

She said, "Did you have fun yesterday?"

I nodded. "Did you?"

"Uh-huh. We went swimming and to McDonald's for lunch. Did you go on the pirate ship?"

"Just for a little while. We went on all the slides and in the wave pool."

"Will you take me there later this summer?"

"Maybe. If you let me go back to sleep."

She settled down, and I thought my bribe might actually work for once. Then she said, "I saw you from the window last night kissing Keith."

I opened my eyes again. Man, she was a pain. "So?"

"So is he like your boyfriend now, or what?"

"Go away, Ali. Wake up Mom and Dad."

Mom laughed from the doorway and echoed Ali. "So is Keith like your boyfriend now or what?" She came in and sat on the edge of my bed. Ali moved over and Sylvester wound up in my face again.

"What is this? The family bed?" I sat up and pushed Sylvester off me.

Mom pulled Ali out from under the covers. "Ali, go downstairs. Dad is making pancakes."

"But I wanna stay." Boy, can she whine.

"Go. I want to talk to Miranda." Mom slid into Ali's spot, plumped up the pillow, and sat back.

"What?" I groaned, sliding back into bed and putting the pillow over my head.

Mom moved the pillow away from my face. "Did you make plans to see Keith again?"

"We didn't really talk about it. But, yeah, probably."

She smoothed my hair along my temple. "Ryan just left for college. I'm not sure getting right back into another relationship is what you need."

"It's not a relationship. We're just hanging out."

"Miranda. Holding hands and good-night kisses are more than just hanging out."

"Okay. Okay. So maybe it's more than hanging out. He's a nice guy."

"I like him too. I'm just saying to take it slow."

"I know, Mom. I'm not stupid, and I'm not a baby."

She touched my cheek with the back of her hand. "You need to put something on this burn so it doesn't peel."

I opened my eyes. "Are we finished with this? I'd like to sleep past seven at least one day this summer."

She sighed. "Just take it easy."

"Whatever, Mom." I closed my eyes, thinking that would make her go away faster. I knew exactly what she meant, even if she wasn't saying it. And I didn't want to talk about it. After she left the room, I jumped up. I needed to get out of there—away from pesky little sisters, mother-daughter chats, and everyone's eyes on my life. I threw on some clothes and headed for Tasha's.

Tasha lived about three blocks away in the top two floors of an old, divided Victorian house. College kids migrated in and out the basement every fall and spring. I let myself in with a key hidden behind dried red chilis hanging on the front porch. The bedrooms were upstairs, but I was quiet crossing the living room where Carly and Josiah were curled up on the couch under an old tattered quilt. I knocked once lightly on Tasha's bedroom door and opened it. She was sitting up in bed, painting her nails and listening to the radio playing quietly next to her. She grinned. "I've been waiting for you to call since last night. Thought you eloped."

"Not a bad idea. At least I wouldn't have to wake up to Ali every morning." I sat on the floor and started rummaging through a basket of nail polish bottles. Tasha's room was nothing like mine. Each wall was dedicated to the four important areas of her life. Music, sports, friends, and fashion. The windows were covered, and she had a lava lamp and a tropical fish tank. Used college textbooks were spread out on the floor. Biology. She figured her only way out of a ramshackle house was winning the lottery or studying. Radio contests were a hobby. She called them her "contingency plan".

Tasha handed me the polish remover from her nightstand. "So?"

"So. So it was great. He is sweet and sexy. I had a blast. Did you have fun with Mack?" I asked the question tentatively, thinking she'd given up the whole day to hang out with my brother for me.

"Mack is a lot more fun than you give him credit for, Miranda.

But now I want to hear details."

"I don't know. We mostly just hung out and talked. I love his voice. It's really deep."

She rolled her eyes. "His voice. What about his body? Did he ever take off his shirt?"

"Oh. My. God." And I pretended to faint. Then I sat back up. "He's got a tattoo. I think it's Japanese. It means harmony."

"Was that the name of his last girlfriend?" she teased.

"No, like peace, you dork. Isn't that cool?"

"Original, anyway." She smiled, slowly. "A tattoo and a motorcycle. Your mama's gonna love that."

I rolled my eyes. "What she doesn't know won't kill her."

"Good point. Did your parents meet him?"

"Yeah. He had dinner with us. They seemed to like him."

"Well, he's got to be better than Ryan. I never got that whole thing with you and him."

"I know. Most of the time I didn't get it either."

"I think it was the sex. Carly says it makes you stupid."

I let that go by without comment. Carly had a right to that opinion. She'd taken me to the birth control clinic the first time. She was huge, pregnant with Josiah then, and warned me I could never be too careful. I chose a polish out of the basket. It was called Faded Denim. "Wonder how you get a job naming nail polish colors?"

Tasha laughed. "I wonder how much a job like that would pay. Nice way to change the subject, Miranda."

Sex was the one thing I hated talking about with Tasha. I already knew we didn't share the same opinions. She wasn't letting any high school silliness drag her down. When I told her about my first time with Ryan, she put her hand up and said, "Don't come crying to me when you realize what a mistake that is. And don't be a fool about it." I started painting my left index finger. The color was lighter than the bottle. I held up my hand. "Keith's eyes are this color."

Tasha threw her pillow at me. "He sounds like a nice boy for a change. Are you going to be able to deal with that?"

I threw the pillow back at her, harder than I needed to. I had to restart my nails.

Tasha put the pillow behind her head. "Look, Miranda, I'm sorry. Ryan was such a jerk. I know you think you know what you are doing, but get to know this guy first."

"I haven't done anything with him yet," I said, blowing on the wet polish. "You and Mom act like I'm the slut of the century."

"Not the century." She tilted her head and asked too casually, "Your mom talked to you?"

"Not exactly, but I got the hint."

"I think she knew about Ryan." She held her hand out for the polish remover.

I passed it over. "Really? She never said anything."

"She almost did to me one time. But then your dad or Mack or somebody interrupted and she changed the subject."

"What?" I stared at Tasha, then put the brush back into the bottle. "When? What exactly did she say?"

Tasha shifted on the bed, her cheeks getting a little pink. "One day over spring break I went over to see you, and you were with Ryan. Your mom apologized that you weren't there. And I kind of laughed and said something like, 'I'm just sorry that Miranda is wasting her time with that loser when she could be hanging out with me.' "

That's so Tasha. "And what did Mom say?"

"Well, she laughed and invited me in. Ali was watching cartoons and your mom was folding some laundry. I helped her with the clothes, and we talked about school and that kind of thing and then when we were carrying the clothes upstairs she goes, 'Tasha, I need to ask you something. Are Miranda and Ryan—' And then Mack came out of his room and I don't know, she never finished asking."

I tried to replay spring break in my head. Mom had wanted me to go skiing with her and I'd backed out, saying I wanted to spend it with Ryan since it was our last break together. She hadn't made a big deal out of it, but she didn't go skiing either. I squinted at Tasha. "She could've been asking about anything."

She shook her head. "Could've. But I don't think so. You had to be there."

I couldn't believe Mom would think I was having sex and not say anything about it. It must be something else. I wondered what, though. I took the brush back out of the bottle. "Why do you suppose she's so hesitant to talk about it with me?"

"You're not honestly asking that question, are you, Miranda, 'Miss Independent, I'm Old Enough to Make My Choices, Thank You Very Much' Watson? Jeez, you scare the hell out of her. You scare the hell out of me." She leaned forward hugging one of her pillows. "You ever think about talking about it with her first?"

"Yeah, right. That's a conversation I want to have." I began a second coat of polish. "With Keith, it's going be different. I can tell. He's the shy type."

"Yeah, I could see that shy side of him when y'all were slow-dancing at the concert."

I laughed. "Come on, Tash, you know what I mean. He's not all polished and smooth."

"You mean he's not like Ryan."

I didn't answer that. I held out both my hands. They looked pretty good. I keep my nails short, but my fingers are long and thin, so my nails appear longer than they are.

"Nice." There was a knock on the door and Tasha's mom looked in. Josiah slipped under her arm and bounded on to the bed. Tasha held her hands up so the polish wouldn't get messed up. Bev is only thirty-four, ten years younger than Mom, but that's not evident from the deep lines etched around her eyes and mouth. "Hi, Miranda. I didn't know you were here. Thought Tasha was talking to herself again."

I stood up but held my hands carefully with my fingers apart. "Sorry if I woke you. I need to get home anyway. I'm supposed to help out with my sister this week." Tasha's clock said eight.

"Stay. You didn't wake me up. I have to be at work soon anyway. Is the iron in here, Tash?"

"No, Carly was using it last."

She waved at us and shut the door.

"I really do need to go. Why don't you come over later?"

"Okay." She put her arm around Josiah. "I'm going to watch the monster while Carly looks for a job. So, later this afternoon probably. You can tell me what Prince Charming says after you call him."

Prince Charming. Tasha knows me too well.

seven

Keith Martin was charming that summer. And I spent every moment completely enchanted.

We were like two little kids trying to get in every bit of summer fun. He would think of things to do that I'd done a hundred times, but make them into new discoveries. Hiking up to Boulder Falls, a small mountain waterfall just off a canyon highway, Keith showed me a path away from the tourists. In warm weather, Boulder Falls is a cool spot, where tourists take snapshots, dogs lap water, rock climbers scale the rock cliffs, and college girls in bikinis float on inner tubes. But we ate our peanut butter and jelly sandwiches alone on top of the world with the sound of the water rushing around us.

On the university campus near a path I'd jogged a million times, he showed me a raccoon den hidden in the brush. I'd come home from work and he'd be shooting baskets with Mack or helping Dad clean the grill or playing Connect Four with Ali. He'd smile at me with his pale blue eyes sparkling.

I spent a lot of time at his ranch, too. It was only ten miles out of the city, but like another world. The house, built over an original homestead, sprawled on one level with spacious views of the mountains to the west and the Denver skyline to the east. There were horses and dogs and kittens and wildflowers. And music. I'd never been around so much music before.

Keith's mom spent a lot of time at a baby grand piano in the living room. She kept her head bowed over the keys, concentrating on the complicated pieces she'd play from memory. When I came over, she'd always flash me a smile and take a break to find out how I was and what our plans were for the day. She's the one who told me that Keith could play the piano, the violin, the guitar, and the saxophone.

Keith's dad was shy and didn't say much but always waved to me from the arena where he trained young horses. When I brought Ali along, he gave her sugar cubes to give to the horses. Once, he showed us where one of the barn cats had hidden her kittens.

Tasha and Mack liked to come out to the ranch, too. Keith had a batting cage near one of the pastures and a pool table in the den. Tasha liked pool. She said it was mathematical. Tasha and Mack would discuss the laws of physics and make bets on their shots.

But I loved most the times I spent alone with Keith.

On the Fourth of July, the two of us hiked up the ridge behind his house so we could see fireworks from all over. We spread our blanket on top of a large boulder and stood next to each other looking over the valley. It wasn't dark, but the sky had that deep purple color it gets sometimes on hot summer nights before becoming black and starry.

Keith put his arm around me. "This is my favorite place."

I moved closer to him. "It's beautiful."

Keith was private with displays of affection. And controlled. He'd hold my hand or throw an arm over my shoulders in front of others, but we were always alone before he'd really kiss me. He was always gentle, and even when we were alone on a blanket far away from interruptions, he kept his hands on my face or my waist or in my hair. I closed my eyes and lost myself to the warmth of his touch and wanted more. I'd have to stop, lay my head against his chest. Breathe. I could hear his heart beat, feel his sweat through his T-shirt.

"My mom had a fit about us coming up here alone tonight," he told me.

"Really?" I sat up, leaning back on my elbows. "Is she worried that I'm going to corrupt her little boy?" I was teasing, but I really hoped that she didn't think that. I liked Keith's parents and wanted them to like me.

He laughed, but then turned pink. "You're the first girl I've ever brought home. I think Mom's kind of freaked out about it."

I wondered if maybe that's why he was so cautious. "How come I'm the first?"

"Up until this summer Dad's always had me on some horse or at baseball camp or Mom's had me practicing concertos in my spare time." He sat up. His hair was bleached lighter by the sun, and it was growing out of the short prep cut he'd had when I first met him.

"What's changed about this summer? You still do all those things."

He hesitated. "I guess I never met a girl I liked as much as you."

I couldn't help liking that.

We stared at the sky. He put his arm around me again, and I leaned back against him, letting him hold me. We watched the Fourth fireworks in silence. "I want to ask you something, but I don't want you to get mad," he said softly next to my ear.

"Promise." I kissed his hand, but didn't turn around to face him.

"Did you have sex with your old boyfriend?"

I knew the question was coming, but now it was my turn to hesitate. I didn't want my answer to change what was going on between us. I closed my eyes, glad that he couldn't see my face. "Yeah, I did."

"Look at me, Miranda." I shifted, turning in his arms. "I thought maybe you had. You're so sure of yourself when we're together. And Mack told me what a jerk he was."

"Mack knows?"

"Well, he didn't say that he did, but he hates him. I have a sister, remember? That's how I'd feel if it were Jody."

I turned back around to watch a huge spray of red, yellow, and orange fireworks.

"Hey," Keith said, hugging me, "don't be mad. You promised."

I took a deep breath. "I'm not mad," I said, pulling away and facing him. Our eyes were accustomed to the dark, but I was still glad that we weren't having this conversation in the daylight. I was going to ask him if he had ever been with anyone, but he wasn't finished.

Keith took my hands. "Jody got raped at a fraternity party when I was fourteen. She was seventeen. She made me promise then that I'd always let the girl tell me when she was ready."

"Is Jody okay now?"

Keith shook his head. "It messed her up. She got a scholarship to Oklahoma for music, but her grades suck. She's in Nashville this summer playing fiddle in a band trying to break into the scene down there. She never used to be reckless like that. She doesn't want to come home. I miss her."

I put my arms around his neck. He held me tightly. It was hard for me to know what to say. But I was glad that we weren't talking about me.

He pulled away first. "Am I scaring you off being all emotional?"

I shook my head. "Girls like guys to be sensitive. Don't you ever read *Cosmo*?"

He laughed. "I forgot to renew my subscription."

The fireworks had tapered off, but there were about a million stars over us. Keith looked at the glowing dial on his watch. "We should go."

"Okay." But neither of us made a move to get up. "I'm good with taking things slowly," I told him. "That's what Tasha thinks I need to do."

"Tasha." He shook his head. "She's not afraid to say what she thinks. Wish I was more like that."

I smiled. "Sometimes I don't need to hear everything she's thinking."

Keith smiled at me. I couldn't see his dimples in the shadows, but I kissed him where the left one was. Another burst of fireworks went off. Pale blues and pinks. We kissed one last time. It was more magical than ever.

eight

For as long as I can remember, the July days after the Fourth seemed to be too hot and too long. I would sit up in the lifeguard chair and watch the waves of heat rise off the cement and sort of wish for school and fall sweaters. But with Keith around, August came before I was ready. Since seventh grade, Tasha and I had always gone to Crossroads Mall on August seventh, Mack's birthday, and shopped for the clothes we were going to wear on the first day of school. It was sort of premature back-to-school shopping, but the summer sales were huge then. We were always back in time for Dad's famous chocolate birthday cake.

This year was going to be different. Since we had our own transportation, we decided to drive to the factory outlets at Castle Rock, south of Denver. Mack and Keith were coming along. Mack was the one who asked if he could go, saying he wanted new cleats and thought he could get a deal there. I only said yes because I knew Mom and Dad would be more receptive to us driving an hour and a half away if Mack or Carly were along. And if Mack was coming, Keith might as well come, too.

At the last minute Keith called. "I'm sorry, Miranda, but I'm not going be able to make it."

He didn't say why. And I didn't ask, even though I wanted to. Instead, I said, "It's not a big deal. It's just shopping. Are you going to be able to make it for cake around five?"

"I don't think I'll be finished then, but why don't you guys meet me at Pearl Street around seven, and I'll take you to Ben and Jerry's."

"Okay. I'll see you later."

Tasha was there when I got off the phone, and she had Josiah with her.

"Carly is working today. Mom was going to watch him, but she's got a migraine. I told Carly to figure something else out, but she threw twenty bucks on the table and walked out." Tasha was not happy.

Mack lifted Josiah high in the air and then pretended to drop him. Josiah wanted to do it again.

"I could kill Carly." Tasha didn't mind watching Josiah, but she liked to be consulted about it first.

Mack said, "He can hang out with Keith and me."

Tasha smiled at him. "That's a swell birthday present for you."

I broke in. "Keith can't come."

"Why?" Tasha asked.

I shrugged. "I didn't ask. He wants to meet us for ice cream tonight instead."

Mack put Josiah on his shoulders. "Well, maybe I should just stay home, too, then. I can keep Jo. I'm sure Ali will love to play with him when she wakes up. She'll get to be the oldest for a change."

"Are you sure?" Tasha asked him. "At least let me give you the twenty bucks."

"Are you crazy? You need to get my birthday present with that. I do not want gum again." Tasha always gave Mack the kind of bubble gum that came in the pouches like chewing tobacco. She said she was getting him ready for the big leagues.

"Well, let's go," I told Tasha, "before Mom figures out the guys aren't coming and decides we don't need to go clear to Castle Rock to buy T-shirts."

I tossed Tasha the keys to the Jeep in the driveway; I knew driving would take her mind off Carly. For a while we drove without speaking, listening to the radio. Then Tasha turned down the volume. "I love Mack. You're so lucky to have a brother like him. I don't know why I let Carly get to me like that." She looked over at me. "I hate that she just walks out and leaves Josiah like that."

I didn't say anything. I'd heard it all before. She looked over at me. "God, Miranda, I hope you're being careful."

"You know I will be, but it's not really an issue yet."

"Really?" she glanced over at me, then looked back to the road. We were merging on to the interstate . Tasha moved into one of the center lanes and slowed almost to a stand still in the morning traffic.

I shrugged. "Really. We're taking it slow." I put my hands up and hung on to the roll bar.

"That's good." I couldn't see Tasha's eyes behind her sunglasses, but I knew the surprise was there. "Why?" she asked.

"All those times with Ryan, and I'm not sure I even really liked him." I let go of the roll bar and looked at the vehicle in the lane next to me, thinking of the words to explain how I felt. I looked back at Tasha. "Keith is different. I want it to be right this time."

She nodded and gave me a smile. "I always knew you'd out-grow your shallow stage."

I smiled back. At least she didn't say "I told you so."

Shopping was more fun without the guys. We pretended we were fashion models and posed like MTV stars while we were trying on clothes. I got new shoes, black jeans and a pale pink tank top that showed off my tan. Tasha bought a yellow shirt with "Charm School Reject" in black letters. She bought Mack a Gap T-shirt with a baseball mitt and glove on the front for three dollars and ninety-nine cents and the pouch of gum. After iced mocha lattes at Starbucks, we drove home singing with the radio, making it back just in time for Dad's chocolate cake. It had been a great day, but I couldn't wait to see Keith.

Pearl Street Mall is crowded on summer evenings. Stores prop open their doors, an invitation to the tourists. Kids looking like they stepped out of the sixties sit on the sidewalks or play hacky sack. Crowds gather around magicians, sketch artists, and a man who makes balloon animals for donations. Mack, Tasha, and I had grown up within blocks of that mall and were used to all the colors and noises and strangeness that attracts newcomers, but we still liked to hang out there once in a while.

"Where did Keith say to meet him?" Mack asked.

We were standing by the entrance of the ice cream store. "He said he'd take us to Ben and Jerry's, but I guess he didn't say he'd meet us here." I looked down the block. There was a small crowd of tourists listening to a street musician a few doors down. "Maybe he's listening to the music." We started in that direction. The song was one I hadn't heard before, but the voice blending with the guitar stopped me. I touched a guy on the shoulder, so he'd make room for us to see.

Keith was sitting on a stool with a guitar, playing requests. With stubble on his cheeks and a ragged bandanna tied round his head, he even looked like a rock star. He wasn't wearing a shirt and the tattoo on his shoulder looked mysterious. His guitar case was open on the sidewalk with a bunch of dollar bills inside. When he saw us, he flashed his dimples at the crowd. "This is for my girl over there." He nodded in my direction.

The song was the ballad that we had danced to at the concert. Tasha stood next to me. "No wonder you're in love."

I was in shock, but I couldn't take my eyes off him. I'd heard him hum and sing along with the radio but had no idea he was so good. My guess was that no one else in his life knew about this. I wondered what it meant that he was sharing it with me.

After the last chord, he jumped off the stool, "Show's over, folks. Thanks for your contributions."

The crowd cleared off and Mack started laughing. "I can't believe this, man."

Tasha said, "You go, boy."

I just shook my head and smiled, too stunned to speak.

Keith pulled on a T-shirt. "Come on, let's get some ice cream. My throat's ready for some."

While we were waiting in the long line, Keith took my hand. "You're not mad that I didn't go shopping, are you?"

I shook my head. "I thought you were busy with something on the ranch. I had no idea."

"It's something I like to do sometimes. I haven't done it this summer though, because I've been afraid that Tasha or you might be hanging out, and I wasn't sure what you'd think. But I've missed it."

We sat on the lawn at the courthouse with our ice cream, watching people go by. Tasha and Mack sat together a few feet away giving Keith and me some privacy.

I leaned back on my elbows in the grass and kicked off my shoes.

"So what do you think?" Keith asked. He was sitting cross-legged like a little boy.

"I'm blown away. Does your mom know you can sing like that?"

He picked a blade of grass and put in it in his teeth. "Yeah, but my dad always said no way was I going to be an opera singer. So she focused on Jody's violin talent and sort of left me to my dad. I don't think either one of my parents would be thrilled to know I'm out here singing for spare change."

I put my foot on his knee. "I thought it was pretty damn sexy."

"Yeah, right." He blushed and looked over at Mack and Tasha. "Those two are getting along well."

Mack was lying on his stomach in the grass and Tasha was laughing at something he'd just said.

"They are getting along well." I thought about how quickly Mack had volunteered to take Josiah. I couldn't believe I hadn't noticed how weird that was. Tasha was my best friend. I thought we told each other everything. I looked at Keith, tilting my head. "Do you know what's going on there?"

Keith shook his head. "I think they're just hanging out, but they'd be good together."

I could see that he was right, but I wasn't ready to think about that. Instead I concentrated on enjoying the warm evening air, the smell of the grass, and the gentle touch of Keith's callused hand around my ankle. Princess Miranda and the Rock Star. That was a twist I hadn't dreamed of before.

nine

Boulder's population swells at the end of August; thousands of college students crowd the streets, and even if the temperatures are still in the nineties, summer seems over. Keith and I did our best to ignore the thought of returning to school and planned a hike for the last day of summer vacation. But at the last minute, Mom told me she had some appointments on campus and she would need my help with Ali. I really think she was just nervous about Keith and me spending our last day of freedom alone on a mountaintop. So we ended up hanging out at my house with Ali, who was packing and repacking her first grade supplies a thousand times.

"I'm sorry," I told Keith. We were sitting on the railing of the deck watching Ali tap-dance.

"It's fine." He took my hand. "Let's go sit over there."

We shared mom's lounge chair, with me sitting in front leaning back against his chest, his arms wrapped around my waist. Ali didn't comment, she just moved her act in front of us again. I sighed. Keith laughed and squeezed me up against him, giving me a kiss on the shoulder.

"Ali," I said, "Do you want an ice cream sandwich? You can have one if you go get it."

She raced off, and I tilted my head around to steal a real kiss. Ali was back in a minute with the whole box. "You guys want some?"

We shook our heads, and she raced off to put the ice cream away. We kissed again, and this time I slipped my hand underneath his T-shirt.

He opened his eyes and smiled.

"Let's play Monopoly," Ali said, slamming the screen door.

I pulled my hand away and turned back around, settling against Keith again. "You want to watch a movie, Ali?"

"Are you going to watch it too?" She was skeptical.

"Sure," Keith told her. I groaned and put my head on my knees. Keith got up and held out his hand. "Come on, Miranda."

"What kind of movies do you like?" Ali asked Keith, opening the video cabinet in the den.

"Long ones," he told her.

I grinned at him and stretched myself out on the couch. He smiled back, but sat on the floor in front of me. Ali chose *The Sound of Music* and flopped down on her stomach on the carpet. We watched the long trailer, and I put my hand on Keith's shoulder. He looked at me and whispered, "Sit with me so I can hold you."

I shook my head. "You come up here."

Keith looked over at Ali. She was engrossed in the film. He got up, and I made room for him on the couch. He stretched out behind me. His hand fell on my bare stomach. I reached up and ran my fingers through his cornsilk-smooth hair.

The screen door slammed shut. Keith and I jumped up as Josiah came tearing into the den. Tasha followed. "Looks like the baby-sitters need some baby-sitting."

I rolled my eyes but sat up. "Hey, Tash."

Josiah had already settled next to Ali, his thumb in his mouth. Tasha got comfy in Dad's recliner. I shook my head. "I guess I'll go make some popcorn."

Mack came home during the "I am sixteen going on seventeen" song. He took one look at the screen and chortled, "Your song, Miranda and Keith." He collapsed in a fit of laughter on the couch next to me. I'd never been so embarrassed in my life and put a pillow over his face, wondering why murdering your brother was a capital offense.

When the song was finally over and Mack had settled down, he held out his hand "Where's my popcorn?"

I threw one piece in his direction.

Tasha laughed. "Here Mack, you can have the rest of mine." She held out her bowl toward him.

"At least someone in this room loves me."

Tasha laughed. "You wish, baby."

Were they actually flirting in front of me? I looked at Keith, my eyebrows raised. He shrugged his shoulders.

Mom came home before the movie was over. Ali and Josiah had fallen asleep. The rest of us were still watching, although for the life of me I couldn't figure out why. Keith and I weren't alone again until the sun was setting and we were sitting out on the curb by his motorcycle, saying good-bye.

"So much for spending our last day together," I said, pulling up a handful of grass.

Keith put his hand around my wrist, and I let the blades fall from my fingers. "It's all right, babe. I had fun anyway."

I put my head against his shoulder.

"Really, Miranda, I did. And," he hesitated. I looked at him. "And maybe it's good we weren't alone today." He blushed.

I smiled. "And here I am thinking you're so polite."

"Doesn't mean I don't think about what we could be doing."

I put my bare foot on top of his sneaker. "What have you done before?"

He blushed again. "Nothing really. I've had girlfriends, but I've never done more than make out a little."

"Does it bother you that I've had sex?" I held my breath, waiting for his answer. I'd wanted to know for a long time.

He shook his head. "No, but I'm afraid you're going to think I don't know what the hell I'm doing."

I took a deep breath. "I wish I'd waited for you, but I had no idea. I didn't know what it was like to be in love before."

He studied my eyes. I could feel tears welling, heavy on my eyelashes. If I blinked, they'd spill over my cheeks in a rush. He put his arm around me and pulled me close. "I didn't mean to make you cry." He rested his chin on my head and stroked my cheek with his finger. "I'm just scared. I don't want to mess up something really good."

I put my head against his chest and closed my eyes for a minute. "Okay. I hear what you're saying."

"I do love you." He kissed me long and slow.

I wished summer never had to end.

ten

I never sleep well before the first day of school, and dreams of Keith filling my head didn't help. I was kind of worried about heading back into the suffocation of high school social life. I had spent two years as the girlfriend of a football hero. I always knew how shallow it was, but I didn't know how school was going to be for me now that Ryan was out of the picture. Would I still have the status? Did I even want it? Over the summer I realized how much of my real self I'd given up to be the person hanging on Ryan's arm. The status I had as a cool girl was something I thought I needed, but now I wasn't so sure. It was a lot of pressure to live up to, being on display all the time. Maybe with Ryan gone, I could slip back into the crowd and have a chance to be myself.

It would have been easier if I had more classes with Tasha; she never cared about the social stratification system. But we had only one class all day together although she had practically the same schedule as Mack. They were on the college track, but I was finished with the minimum science and history requirements, so I was taking ceramics and advanced drawing. Mom and Dad threw a fit about my schedule. I could have kept up in the classes Mack and Tasha were taking, but I didn't want to dissect worms and write essays about ancient civilizations.

The worst thing about going back to school, though, was the thought of being away from Keith all day, every day. So I was up before daylight, sitting cross-legged on my bed, and choosing pictures of him to tape inside my locker. If I couldn't spend the day with him, at least I could see his smile whenever I needed to.

Mom saw my light on and came in dressed for a work. She liked jeans but mostly wore long skirts and tailored shirts to her lectures. She had early classes and usually was gone before we left for school, even on the first day. "Hi, baby. Ready for today?"

I shrugged. "Guess so." I didn't think it would do any good to tell her I couldn't believe I had to face slamming lockers and clanging bells when all I wanted was sunlight and Keith.

Mom sat down on the bed and picked up one of the photos from the reject pile. It was one Tasha had taken of Keith and me at the pool. Keith was holding me on his lap in a beach chair. There was a lot of blue in the picture. The sky, our eyes, the water, my bikini. Mom put it down without looking at the rest of them. "Is that what you're wearing to school?"

I had on cute jean shorts with daisies embroidered on the hip pockets and the pale pink tank top I'd bought with Tasha on our summer shopping trip.

"Is this appropriate?" Mom asked, touching the skinny strap of the tank top. It just covered my pink bra strap.

It wasn't, but it was adorable and looked great with my dark tan. All the cool junior and senior girls defied the dress code the first week of school, and even if I wanted a lower profile, not going along with the crowd on this issue would gain me even more attention. I knew I could never explain that to Mom though, so I just said, "I'll wear a shirt over it," figuring that would appease her. "I'm going to hang out with Tasha after school, if that's okay."

Mom nodded. "Be home by six. You know the dinner thing." The dinner thing. Another annoying Watson tradition. We almost always ate dinner together, but on the first day of school it was like this big celebration, with candles and salad forks. Ali told us all about elementary school. Mack was always excited about upgrades in the tech system. I just tried not to yawn.

Mom leaned over and kissed me on the cheek and then stood up. "Miranda, choose a new outfit. I do not want to get a call that you need appropriate clothing today."

"You won't," I assured her. The first week of school the teachers just reminded us of the dress code. I figured I could get away with some apologies and "I won't wear it again" if anyone even noticed in the first-day madness of everything.

By the time the first bell rang, I wished I had listened to Mom and changed my shirt. The tank top looked too good. Suddenly all of Ryan's football buddies remembered that I was supposedly a free woman. Or else unclaimed property. With the whistles and attention I was getting, it wasn't too hard to guess what Ryan had told them.

Mike Jergens, a big linebacker, backed me against my locker. "Looking good, Watson." He put his big, sweaty paw on my shoulder, sliding the tank strap off my shoulder. "Meet me after practice."

"Yeah, right," I told him, ducking under his arm. But I was glad Algebra 2 was only two doors away from my locker. I slid into a seat between Mack and Tasha. My hands were shaking.

The teacher was new to the school—a young, skinny guy with a Bugs Bunny tie. He asked if Mack and I were twins. It's a tradition for at least one teacher a year to ask us that question. Mack and I nodded and the rest of the class laughed. The teacher looked around, not getting the joke, and then mispronounced the next name on the list. Tasha took advantage of the slow roll call and passed me a note:

"Saw Paleo-brain giving you a hard time. You okay?"

I folded it back up and nodded yes. I didn't want Mack getting into a fight with the biggest guy in school. Even though I hate math, I was sorry when the bell rang and I had to go to English by myself.

The only good thing about English was that it was an honors class and there wasn't a chance that any of Ryan's friends would show up there. But Mrs. McDonald was the kind of teacher who noticed juniors trying to slide around the dress code the first day of school. I sat in the back row and tried to disappear into the wall, but Mrs. McDonald, who had also taught my freshman English class, singled me out to read a poem from the textbook. And then, just before the bell rang, she asked me to stay for a minute.

"Nice tan, Miranda," she said when the class had cleared out.

"Thanks," I said, sweet as pie. "I'm sure you won't be seeing quite as much of it from now on."

She was also the kind of teacher who could laugh at something like that. "I'm sure that I won't be. Did you do any painting over the summer?"

I shrugged and got up from the desk, picking up my notebook. "Some." After an afternoon riding with Keith, I'd done a watercolor of his horse in a field of sunflowers. When Keith first saw it, he stared for a long time, holding it by the edges. After I gave it to him, he had it framed.

Mrs. McDonald broke into my thoughts. "I could use a hand with set design for some of the productions this year."

She'd asked me once before and I'd turned her down because the "theater crowd" didn't mix with Ryan's crowd, but now I said, "I could probably help."

"Good. I'll let you know when we start." She nodded toward the door. "I think your friend is waiting for you."

Tasha was leaning against the frame. "Busted."

Mrs. McDonald laughed. "See you tomorrow, girls."

Tasha and I sat on the front steps of the building, waiting for Mack. His locker was on the other side of the building from his last class. Jessie, Mary Anna, and Eden, girls we hung out with at school, were sitting with us, catching up on summer stuff. Tasha put her hand on my shoulder. "Look, there's Keith."

He had pulled over to the curb at the side of school where the buses were pulling away. He waved. He wasn't wearing a helmet, and his hair was windblown. Jessie whistled. "Jeez, Miranda. No wonder you've been hiding out with him all summer."

I turned to Tasha. She held out her hand and I handed her my backpack. "Thanks. Tell Mack I've got a ride home." I didn't run across the lawn, although it was hard not to.

"I was hoping I'd see you," Keith said, putting his hand on my waist and giving me a light, easy kiss.

The girls on the step cheered. A guy walking by gave us a look and said, "Oh I get it, Watson, Central High guys aren't good enough for you anymore." He had played football with Ryan and I knew him from parties. He was a jerk and I ignored him.

But Keith said, "Come on, let's get out of here."

His motorcycle was one of those Ninja rockets, the kind that leans forward and requires the passenger to really hold on to the driver. I loved that bike. I swung on behind Keith, pressing close and wrapping my arms around his stomach, laying my cheek against his back. He touched me once on the thigh, then steered into a side street to escape the slow, heavy stream of traffic. I didn't care where we went.

At Boulder Falls Keith took his backpack that he had hooked over the handle bars and nodded at my shoes. "Are you going to be able to hike in those?"

I had on pale pink flip-flops. Even my feet were tan and I had painted my toenails that Faded Denim color from Tasha's nail polish basket. The color was exactly the same shade as Keith's eyes. "How far are we going?"

"Just up on the rocks, away from the people."

"I think I can handle it. What's in the backpack?"

He smiled like a little kid with a secret. "It's a surprise."

I rolled my eyes. He laughed and took my hand. We headed for Boulder Falls and the rocks above and beyond the falls, close enough to hear the creek and see it winding down the canyon but far away from the sounds of the crowd. On a nice flat rock ledge, we stopped and Keith pulled a blanket out of the pack. I grinned. "What else is in there?"

He smiled and held the pack out of my reach. "Just spread out the blanket, why don't you?"

I did, then lay back on it and stretched my arms over my head. Keith joined me, putting his hand on my stomach and kissing me on the throat, then the mouth.

"Wow. Does school always make you like this?" I teased.

He laughed and sat up. "I just missed you."

I sat up too, and put my hand on his leg. He had on shorts—denim carpenter shorts—the new creases almost visible. We had been in the sun almost every day for three months, and his white-blonde hair made his tan seem even darker than mine. "I am really glad you came to pick me up today," I said.

"Me too." He put his hand on top of mine. "How was school?"

I considered. I didn't want to get into it. I played it safe and shrugged. "I hate being away from you."

He squeezed my hand and gave me a kiss. We sank back onto the blanket again.

I closed my eyes and concentrated on the sound of the roaring creek, the warm sun on my skin, Keith's gentle hands in my hair. The crowded halls and obnoxious boys faded away. And so did the time.

Shadows had fallen over us when we heard laughter and foot-steps sliding on the rocks. We sat up, and I tugged my tank top down over my stomach and made a sweep through my hair with my fingers. A couple came into view above us. They had to climb onto the boulder we were on to get down the mountain. Keith and I scrambled up and moved the blanket out of their way.

"Thanks," the guy said. They paused and looked out at the view. The creek was dark in the shadows. "Nice spot."

I nodded. "It is." Before I met Keith, I could give great directions to the Gap, but I never really paid attention to the mountains. Now I couldn't believe I'd taken them for granted for most of my life.

"Doing some climbing?" Keith asked, putting his arm around my waist.

The girl shook her head, "Nah. We're just looking around." She winked at us. "We'll let you get back to what you were doing."

Keith blushed, and for once, so did I.

The guy hopped onto the rock below us, then moved out of the way so the girl could follow.

I spread the blanket back out and Keith reached for his back-pack. "Hungry?"

I thought about the dinner thing at home. Dad usually made something fancy—crab quiche or fajitas. I wondered for just a second how much trouble I was going to be in, then I turned my attention to the feast Keith had brought—peanut butter and jelly on wheat, tangerines, honey sticks from the farmer's market and warmish bottled water. It was about the best meal ever, eating on the mountain with the sun setting behind us. I hugged my knees toward my chest and met Keith's eyes. "Let's just stay up here forever."

He grinned. "Okay." He kissed me again, tasting honey-sweet. "I don't have any more food, though. Guess we'd have to eat leaves and berries like the deer do."

I kissed him back, sliding my hands up the back of his shirt. He put his hand on my right shoulder, sliding the skinny strap of the tank top and the silky strap of the bra off onto my arm, just like that jerk Mike had done. "It's getting harder to just kiss," he whispered, kissing me softly below my collarbone and then meeting my eyes.

Part of me wanted to say, "Let's do more, then." But the other part remembered Mike's leer at school. I don't know where the tears came from, but they were there on my cheeks, hot and fast.

Keith immediately took his hands off me. "I'm sorry, baby. What's wrong?"

I took my hands from under his T-shirt. "It's not you, Keith." I bit the inside of my cheek and looked out at the sky. It wasn't dark enough for stars yet, but the moon was visible against the blue. I couldn't look at him. "Ryan must have told the entire football team we had sex. They were all but waiting in line for a turn." I was surprised by the anger in my voice even though I was crying.

Keith didn't say anything, but he wiped off my cheek with his thumb. His callused touch was gentle. "Want to talk about it?"

"Not really." I tried to get myself under control. "I should have known, but I thought two years would have counted for something."

"He sounds like a real jerk. And so do all his buddies." His hand was warm on my face. "Why you were with him for so long?"

I shrugged. "I don't know." But then I was honest. "I guess I was a typical freshman. Naïve. I liked the idea of going out with a junior. Liked the attention. Believed it when he said I was hot. Liked that a lot." I glanced sideways at Keith. "And maybe I was a little afraid to break up with him. I thought he'd make up stuff about me. Tasha always said he was a predator. She was right."

Keith gave me a slow smile and jiggled my knee with his free hand. "You are hot." He kissed the top of my head and stood up, kind of kicking at the rock with the top of his sneaker. "So how old were you the first time?"

"My freshman year. I was fourteen."

He shook his head and gave a low whistle. "He *was* a predator, baby. What a jerk." He stood on the edge of the rock, then turned around. "I know some guys like that. They pick out the good-looking freshman, some even go for seventh- or eighth-graders, just to see what they can get. It usually doesn't last two years."

I stayed where I was, hugging my knees. "I know, but Ryan was selfish. He knew he didn't want anyone else getting what he thought was his. I thought if it was all about the sex for me, too, then we'd be even."

Keith sat next to me but didn't touch me. "You can never be even with a guy who's going to spread stuff around to his buddies."

"Why do guys do that?"

He shrugged. "I don't know. Bragging, I guess."

I put my chin on my knees. "I didn't like how those guys made me feel today. Cheap or something. I never felt that way before."

"That's the idea, I think." He put his hand around my ankle. "Don't believe it for a minute." He let go of my ankle and touched my cheek again. "You know Miranda, bringing you up here today, I don't want you to think—"

Putting my finger to his mouth, I stopped his words. "I know, Keith."

He took hold of my hand and pulled me gently to him. "Let me hold you."

I moved over on the rock and leaned back against him. He moved my hair to the side and kissed the side of my neck and then wrapped his arms around my waist. His voice was serious. "Miranda, did any of those guys touch you today?"

"It was just a lot of talk." That was mostly the truth.

He held me tighter. "Are you sure?"

I tilted my head back and looked at him upside down. "Are you going to do some butt-kicking for me?" I kept my voice light, teasing.

Keith was serious. "Miranda, I know how those guys are. I don't want you getting hurt."

I looked back into the darkness. "I'll be fine. They'll forget about me in a day or two." That was true enough. Most of Ryan's buddies had short attention spans. "I can take care of myself."

He kissed me on the ear. "I know. You're such a big, tough girl."

I laughed. "Okay, I'll stick close to my friends. And I'll say something if it gets bad."

"Promise?"

I nodded and twisted around for a kiss. "You know something, baby? I was supposed to be home hours ago."

"Yeah, me too."

"I wish I could just quit school now."

"That's a great idea. We can get on the bike and ride off into the night."

But we got up and folded the blanket. Keith held my hand tightly down the trail. The porch light went on when we pulled into the driveway, but we held each other close anyway. "I'm going to be in a lot of trouble," I sighed, pulling away.

"I'll go in with you."

I shook my head no. "Your parents are going to be upset, too. You need to go home. I'll be okay."

He squeezed my hand once more. "You be careful tomorrow,

babe."

I watched the red tail lights fade away, took a deep breath, and walked toward the house.

eleven

I seriously considered not going in. I could have walked over to Tasha's and slipped into her room. She probably would have thought staying out all night with Keith was stupid, but she would have understood. But Mack eased open the front door and sat on the porch with me. He was eating a bowl of ice cream. "So where have you been?'

I shrugged my shoulders. "How much trouble am I in?"

He handed me the rest of his ice cream. "Eat up. Might be your last meal."

"Come on, Mack." I handed back the dish.

"Well, Ali was upset that you didn't hear all about her first encounter with Blind Man's Bluff. She's studying pioneers and learning old games. Dad, well, he gets it that you were probably just hanging out with Keith. He thinks you should've called, but he doesn't think you should be grounded for life. That's what Mom is voting for; she is pissed beyond belief."

"Great," I sighed and went into the house.

Dad was in the kitchen kneading dough. He has big hands and his arms were tan and muscular. His veins stood out with the movement. I wondered if he told guys at work that he made bread when he needed to relax. "Sorry I missed dinner," I said, sitting down at the counter. I thought I could sweet-talk Dad out of being mad at me. Sometimes if I pulled out the "daddy's girl" stuff, I could get my way.

Dad turned the bread over in the flour and continued kneading, but glanced at the clock. It was nine o'clock. "What the hell were you thinking?" He asked matter-of-factly, like he was completely puzzled instead of mad.

"I'm sorry, Dad. I just had a really bad day at school. Keith picked me up, and I guess I just forgot about the time. You know, I've never been late before." That was about the lamest excuse ever, but I blinked my eyes to get them to water. Dad hated crying.

He quit kneading the dough and sat on the stool across from me. He had on a blue denim shirt, and it was covered in flour. "Come on, don't cry. We were just worried about you."

Score, I thought, but kept my eyes downcast and ran my finger along the smooth edge of the countertop. Using my best scared, sad, pitiful voice, I asked, "Where's Mom?"

He nodded toward the deck. "She's pretty mad. And hurt. We've given you a lot of freedom, and we didn't expect you to take advantage."

"I know. I'm sorry. I didn't mean to hurt anyone."

"Well, next time you need to call. Go talk to your mom."

He picked up the bread dough again, and I got up and went to the window over the sink. Mom was standing against the railing of the deck facing the house, her arms folded in front of her. I could see her pretty well from the light of the kitchen. She was chewing on her lip. I didn't say anything when I came out because she wouldn't buy any sorry little girl crap.

I stood next to her, keeping my arms folded against my stomach. I still had the tank top on that she had told me not to wear. I knew that wasn't going to win me any points. "Guess you're pretty mad."

Neither of my parents is the screaming type, but Mom's voice had an edge to it when she answered. "Mad isn't even close to how I feel right now." I hoisted myself up on the railing. Mom turned around to face me. "What have you been doing for the last six hours?"

"I was just hanging out with Keith. We've been out later than this tons of times. Really, I don't think it was that big of a deal. I'm sorry everyone's so upset."

70

Mom's eyes pierced into mine. "Not that big of a deal, Miranda? You lied about the shirt, lied about being with Tasha. Not to mention tearing around town on a motorcycle and who knows what else you've been doing all these hours. "

I was getting mad too. "I didn't lie about Tasha. I didn't know Keith was going to come by school. And I didn't lie about the shirt either. I told you that you wouldn't get a phone call. And you didn't, did you?"

"No, I didn't. But you did wear the shirt when I told you not to."

"So ground me for the rest of my life!" Mom hated sarcastic things like that, but I didn't care.

She took a deep breath. She also hated arguing. "Let's start this over. What were you really doing tonight? Please be more specific than hanging out."

"Nothing really. We rode up to Boulder Falls."

"So you were up in the mountains alone. What else were you doing?"

I suddenly got what she thought we had been doing, and if I was upset before, it was nothing to how I felt then. "Nothing."

She looked at me. Her arms still folded in front of her.

"You don't believe me?"

"I want to believe you, Miranda."

I could feel the tears start. I looked out at the dark and blinked them back. I hate that I cry when I'm angry. "Is that what Dad thinks, too?"

She shook her head. "He trusts you."

"And you don't?" I wiped the tears off my cheeks with the back of my hand.

"I don't know anymore. I don't know what to believe."

I slid down off the railing onto the deck. "I don't know what you're talking about, Mom. Maybe you should take another look at those parenting books." My plan after that withering remark was to storm up to my room, but Mom grabbed my wrist.

71

"Don't, Miranda."

She got my attention. My parents weren't the physical type, so for Mom to grab me like that was a big deal. I could've pulled away—she was holding me firmly, but not hurting me—but I didn't. As soon as Mom realized I wasn't going anywhere, she let go.

"This is not how I wanted this conversation to go." She looked up at the sky and looked back at me. "You've always got to be so tough, Miranda. Why?"

I shrugged my shoulders. Keith had called me tough, too. At first it was an act to set me apart from the rest of my family, but it had come in handy with a guy like Ryan around, and now it was second nature. Maybe I didn't need it as much with a boy who sang love songs on street corners—or with my mother when she was close to crying. But I wasn't sure I knew another way.

When I didn't say anything, Mom sighed and sat in one of the deck chairs. "Tell me something, Miranda. Are you sleeping with him?"

I folded my arms and leaned against the deck railing. The night air was cooling off and I was shivering in the tank top. "Does it matter what I say if you're not going to believe me?"

Mom looked at her hands. Her fingers were long like mine. And Mack's. And Ali's. She kept her nails manicured but never wore jewelry. Not even a wedding band. "I know you're not a virgin, Miranda. I've known since February, but my guess is that it's been longer." She didn't look at me.

I knew exactly what she meant. She and Dad had invited my swim team over for a party after our last meet in February. Ryan and I had slipped out onto the deck, thinking we were so sly, copping feels with no one around. Mom had opened the deck door and told us to come inside. I didn't think she had seen anything, but she must have. After the party she had come to my room and sat on the edge of the bed. I had pretended to be asleep. I watched her now looking at her hands. "Why didn't you say something, Mom?"

It was her turn to shrug. "Would it have made a difference?"

"No," I said, sitting in the chair next to hers, "but it's not like that with Keith, Mom. You have to believe me. We're not doing anything."

Finally she looked at me. "For how long? Once you've said yes, it's so much harder to say no. I've seen you two together, the way you look at each other. It scares me."

"Why? Why are you scared? I know about birth control and disease and all that stuff."

"There's so much more to it than that, baby." She got up and leaned against the railing again. I could hear her voice cracking.

"I know that, Mom."

"Do you really, Miranda?" She didn't bother wiping away her tears.

I took a deep breath. "I do. Tasha used to think Ryan was using me. And I guess maybe he was." I thought about the how the boys at school had treated me, but I didn't cry like I had earlier in Keith's arms. "I know he didn't love me, but I didn't love him either."

"And that made it okay?"

I shrugged. "I thought so then. I didn't realize it would hurt like this later." I held my tears back.

Mom wasn't fooled. "This is my fault," she said. "I should have said something. I was just shocked that you were making these choices so soon." She knelt on the deck next to my chair and moved a strand of hair out of my eyes. "I guess I still think of you as my baby."

"I'm not a baby, Mom." But I didn't move away from her touch.

"I know you aren't a baby, Miranda. But I also know what you're like, honey. You always think you can deal with everything by yourself. I can see how you think Keith is the fairy tale come true. I'm just scared you are going to get lost in something you are way too young to be handling."

"I haven't totally lost touch with reality, Mom." I tried a smile. "I'm not going to make the same mistakes again."

She didn't smile. "Okay, Miranda. But when you're in love like you are, it's never going to seem like a mistake. And that's when real mistakes happen."

"I guess we're going to have to trust that I make the right choices then. I think I can, Mom." And I did. I knew what I was doing.

Mom sighed. I could tell she wasn't convinced. She studied me. I knew she didn't know what to say.

"So am I grounded?"

"That's not really the issue, is it?" She got up and walked to the end of the deck. I sat there listening to the sounds of the night—crickets, the neighbor's sprinkling system—waiting her out. After what seemed like hours, she said, "I would ground you, Miranda, if I thought it would do any good." She sat back down in the deck chair and took my hand. "Okay. I'll have to trust you to make good choices. I don't see any other way."

I glanced at the house. I could see Dad in the kitchen window, but he wasn't looking at us. "Are you going to tell Dad?" I hated being thought of as Mom's baby, but I didn't know if I could stand my father knowing I wasn't his innocent little girl anymore.

She shook her head no, let go of my hand and went inside, leaving me alone on the deck. I thought about what she had said about me falling into the fantasy, fairy tale world of love. I wouldn't admit it, but I knew she was right.

twelve

As much as I wanted to forget about school, I couldn't. And I couldn't just disappear, either. Ryan's football buddies were victorious September through October and strutted around worse than ever. I stuck to the dress code and the back row in class, but I was too well-known just to blend in with the human sea in the hallways. And once word got around about Keith picking me up on the motorcycle, the whistles turned into jeers. Mike Jergens lurked around my locker, all proud of himself for handling the ball on the field. He was determined to handle me off of it.

I was scared, but I refused to let anyone know it, especially Mike. Tasha wasn't fooled, though, and tried to get me to tell Mrs. McDonald or another teacher, but I didn't want to make the situation worse. And I was embarrassed about the whole thing. I didn't want teachers knowing that stuff. It was bad enough that Tasha and Mack and my other friends knew what some of the guys were saying about me. The worst part was there was some truth to it all.

One morning, Mack showed up at my locker with some of his books. He told me he was tired of going up to the third floor to his locker when all his classes were on the first floor and he shoved his chemistry book and graphing calculator on the shelf where I keep my makeup. For once, I was grateful to have him around. Those football jerks still talked about me, but Mike Jergens wasn't brave enough to grab me in front of my brother.

Even though having Mack there helped a lot, each day as soon as the two-forty-five bell rang, I bolted from Mrs. McDonald's room and met Keith across the street. Every day while the weather was warm we rode away from the brick walls under the fluttering shower of autumn leaves.

I kept a rein on how far I let the kissing go, partly because I was trying to prove that I could be somewhat responsible, but mostly because just being with Keith was enough. I made it home in time for dinner, did all of my homework, and when I got too entranced by the daily slide into melting kisses, I remembered to make an effort to breathe deeply and slow down.

I didn't share any information with Mom about what Keith and I did after school. I could see she was doing her best to trust me. She didn't ask me any questions, but I could see that it wasn't easy for her. She was biting her nails, a new habit for her, and when she'd check on me at night, she'd smooth my hair behind my ears.

Sometimes when her gentle fingers touched my cheek in the darkness, I almost told her what was happening at school, but I didn't want to add to her worries.

The first cold, bleak, gray day of fall I was sitting in Mrs. McDonald's class, staring out the window as she recited poetry by some guy I never heard of before. I had no clue where Keith and I would go if it started to rain, or worse, snow. The mountains were out and so was my house; Ali was too much of pain to deal with for long. The loudspeaker interrupted the poetry and my thoughts. To my surprise, I was called to the office. Mrs. McDonald raised her eyebrows at me but was reading again before I got out the door.

My friend Jessie was one of the office aides, and she was sitting behind the counter chewing on a pencil.

"What's up?" I asked her. Even though I didn't take school as seriously as Mack and Tasha, I didn't cause any problems. It was the first time I'd ever been called to the office.

She grinned. "Keith came by."

"No kidding? Where is he?" I looked around, but the hall was empty.

"He was shooed away." Jessie nodded toward the secretary on the phone. "She did tell me I could give you the message though."

"Well?"

"He can't pick you up because his parents want him to go with them somewhere after school. He said he didn't know about it til now. Man, he is a hottie, Miranda."

I grinned. "Yep." Leaning on the counter I said, "Think Mrs. McDonald would notice if I didn't go back to class?"

Jessie laughed. "She'd notice. Do you need a ride home?"

"Maybe." I thought I remembered Mack and Tasha mentioning something about studying for a chemistry test, and that meant hours in the library for them. I wanted to go home. Keith would probably call as soon as he could. "Actually, okay. Where should I meet you?"

"Just come by here. I don't need anything from my locker."

The secretary hung up the phone. "Miranda, you have twenty minutes of class left."

"I'm going," I told her. "Thanks for letting me know."

When Jessie dropped me off, the Jeep was already in the drive. Mack was sitting with Ali at the kitchen counter. They were eating orange slices. I sat down with them and took a slice.

"Where's Keith?" Ali asked.

"He had something to do." I might have told Mack about Keith coming by school, but I didn't really know anything, and Ali asked too many questions.

"I would've looked for you after school, but I thought you and Tasha were going to study for chemistry. How did you get here so fast?" I asked my brother.

"Mom had a department meeting, so I left right away."

I felt a twinge of guilt. Mom had those meetings every other week. Mack and I had taken turns watching Ali in previous years, but I hadn't watched her once since going back to school. I sat down at the counter with them. "What are you up to?"

"I want to play Chinese checkers," Ali told me, "but Mack says he has to study for his chemistry test."

"I'll play with you. Why don't you study, Mack?"

"I don't know, Miranda. Are you going to charge out of here if the love of your life calls?" He was teasing, but I deserved it.

"Get out of here before I change my mind," I said.

"I'll be at Tasha's." His voice was nonchalant, but he didn't quite meet my eye.

I knew they were lab partners, but it occurred to me that lately Mack was spending more time with Tasha than I was. I wasn't exactly sure how I felt about that. I watched him cram one more orange slice in his mouth. The juice ran down his chin; he swiped at his face with his hand and left. I turned my attention to Ali, she was even stickier than Mack. "Wash up, Ali, and meet me in my room."

We played a couple of games of checkers, and then I told her I'd read to her for a while if she wanted. Ali could read just fine by herself, but she adored when Mack and I read to her. When I was Ali's age, my favorite story was *Beauty and the Beast*. I still had it on my bookshelf. She chose a book off her shelf and came and sat on the bed with me. She picked out a Junie B. Jones book. She liked how Junie talked and how she was always getting into some kind of trouble. I thought it was kind of silly, but I opened to the first page and Ali laid her head against my arm. She smelled like raspberries.

"You've been in my shampoo, Ali."

She looked up at me to see if I was really mad. "I heard Keith say he liked the way your hair smelled. I wanted to see if it would work for me."

"What are you talking about?" She had my complete attention.

"I sit next to a boy named Daniel at school. He's got really curly red hair, and he let me borrow his eraser once. I thought maybe he would like me if my hair smelled like yours."

I was shocked, but I said, "Did it work?"

"He said I smelled like jelly."

If Mack had been there, I might have laughed, but for some

reason it didn't seem that funny. "I don't think boys notice shampoo until high school."

"Well, what do they notice in first grade?"

I closed my eyes, pretending to think. I opened them back up and said. "First-grade boys notice girls who have their own school supplies."

Ali studied me with her serious brown eyes, making sure I wasn't teasing, and then she settled up against my arm again.

I read the words, but my mind didn't follow the story. I never realized Ali paid that much attention to what I did. I never thought my actions had much impact on her or Mack. I never once considered what it would be like for him to walk into the locker room and hear my name being thrown around. And I certainly didn't want my baby sister following some of my leads. I sure wasn't going to win any prizes for Sister of the Year.

Keith called at four-thirty. "Hi. Can I come over? I have something to show you." I knew what Mack said about abandoning Ali, but I really wanted to see Keith. He always made me feel better.

It turned out that Mom came home right after the phone call anyway. She was so pleased that I had spent some time with Ali that she didn't get that worried look when I said Keith was coming over.

Keith was like a little kid at Christmas. He kissed me as he came in the doorway then told me to cover my eyes. He steered me out to the driveway. The surprise was a new red truck. Shiny chrome wheels, tinted windows, four-wheel drive. I could see why he was so excited even though I never heard him once mention that he wanted a truck.

"It's an early graduation present," he told me, opening the driver's door and motioning me to climb in and check it out. We never discussed the fact that he was a senior and supposed to be thinking about college plans.

Mom and Ali came out to see what the fuss was about. Keith lifted Ali onto the running board, and she climbed in over me.

"Wow. This is very nice," Mom said, walking around the truck and joining us at the driver's door. "Is it brand-new?"

"Three years old. Low mileage, though. I like blue better, but I wasn't about to complain." He put his head on Mom's shoulder. "Please, please, can I take Miranda for a drive?"

Mom laughed. "Okay. A short one. How about around the block?"

"Mom!" I protested.

"Well, you probably have homework, right?"

"I always get it done, don't I?"

She raised her eyebrows. Her definition of finished homework wasn't always the same as mine.

"Come on, Mom. I just have some reading to do for English. I'll do it when I get home. Promise."

"Okay," she said, giving in. "You can go. Don't be late for dinner. Come on, Ali." I expected Ali to whine, and I was all prepared to give in because of our little chat, but she hopped out when Keith opened the passenger door.

"What are you doing?" I asked him.

"You can drive."

"Really?"

He grinned. "Why not?"

I'd never driven anything that new before. I was pretty quiet, concentrating on the heavy evening traffic. Keith fooled around with the buttons on the radio, setting our favorite stations in the memory. When he was finished, he rested his hand on my thigh. "Let's see how well it parks."

I laughed. "Okay." I drove out to the mountain park south of town and pulled into a space away from the few cars parked in the growing darkness. I left the key in the ignition and moved over onto Keith's lap. He slid his hands into my back pockets, something he'd been doing now that I was wearing jeans instead of shorts.

A light drizzle fogged the windows. The radio was playing softly, and I was totally cozy. I put my hands against his cheeks. "I was wondering what we were going to do when the weather got cold."

"Now you know." He pulled me closer and kissed my throat. "How was your day?"

"Better now." I didn't want to talk about school or Mack and Tasha or Ali.

The leather seat was comfortable and there was plenty of space for us to stretch out. It was so easy to slip into his arms, return his kisses, and forget all about the rest of my life.

The darkness slid in, hiding us from the rest of the world. I shifted on Keith's lap, aware of how the movement made him catch his breath. He ran his hands under my T-shirt, fumbling with the hooks of my bra. I shifted again, pressing as close to him as I could.

"We need to stop, baby. We're going to be late," he whispered.

"I know." I kissed both his dimples, then leaned my forehead against his for a moment. Then sighing, I eased off his lap. Stopping was about the last thing I wanted to do. "Maybe nobody would notice if we were a little late."

"I wish." He gave me a last kiss and then started the engine. "Come, sit close to me."

"Like those cowgirls do?" I teased, sliding over next to him and putting my head on his shoulder.

He laughed. "You're not much of a cowgirl, sweetheart." He rested his hand on my thigh for a moment, then put both hands on the wheel. "Should we talk about birth control?"

The question caught me off guard. The "we-ness" of it. Ryan and I hadn't discussed birth control ever. Tasha was the one who made Carly take me to get birth control when nothing she said warned me off of him. I took the shot in my hip every three months. It was good, no pills to forget or to hide from Mom. But when Ryan went away to college, I quit. I thought about going back on it, hoping that the lack of birth control would help me wait, but Keith and I were getting closer every time.

"Don't worry about it. I'll take care of it," I told Keith, putting my hand on his thigh. His jeans were old and smooth.

He put his hand on top of mine. "No, baby. It should be both of us. What did you do before?"

"The shot, but I've been off it since May. I can make an appointment, though."

"I'll go with you if you want."

"Okay." I lay my head against his arm like Ali had done to me earlier. It didn't really surprise me that he wanted to come, but it made me realize that Ryan really had never taken any kind of responsibility. I was lucky Tasha had more sense than I did at the time.

Keith squeezed my hand. "What are you thinking?" he asked.

I bit my lip, glad that he couldn't read my mind. "I didn't go back on birth control because I thought it might help make me wait longer. I really want it to be special." Tasha and Mom probably would have fainted dead away to hear those words come out of my mouth, and to tell the truth, I was kind of shocked myself. "But I can make an appointment. It might take a week or two before I can get in to the clinic."

He squeezed my hand again. "I'm in no hurry, baby. I just want to be safe when we get there."

"I know. Me too," I told him. That was the truth.

When we reached my house, Keith parked in the driveway, and the motion sensors kicked on the outside lights. We were a few minutes late, but I didn't think I'd be in trouble and we always said good-bye in the driveway for awhile.

Keith touched my face. "You're quiet."

Taking a deep breath, I said, "I guess I'm sort of scared. Do you think it'll change things?" Sex hadn't changed my relationship with Ryan, but there really hadn't been anything to change.

Keith brushed my hair from my face. "Look, Miranda. I know you've been hurt. I'd never do that. You know that, right? Let's just hold off on the birth control stuff until you're ready."

I nodded and he held me close.

thirteen

The drizzle lasted the rest of the week, and then it got much colder. I woke Halloween morning to a heavy white blanket against the bare black branches of the tree outside my window. I could hear Ali and Dad in the yard rolling a snow family. It was their tradition. Mack and I usually did everything possible to avoid being part of the festivities. I pulled my fluffy down comforter over my head and prepared to hibernate for a few more hours. Little-kid giggles and my door creaking open pulled me from my dreams. I opened one eye and saw Josiah and Ali sneaking in covered in snow. "Out," I shouted, throwing my pillow at them.

The door flew open and Tasha grabbed Josiah around the middle. "I told you not to come in here."

She shooed both kids out and came and sat on the floor by my bed. She was wearing old jeans and a big fluffy yellow sweater. Her cheeks were red from the cold. She loved the first snow and had come over to help Dad and Ali with their snow family ever since seventh grade. "Hey, Sleeping Beauty."

I smiled at her but didn't sit up. "Thanks for rescuing me."

"Whatever. Are you getting up?"

I looked at the clock. It was nearly noon, but the snow had blocked out the morning light. "Maybe not."

Tasha laughed and tugged the covers off me onto the floor. I sleep in my underwear and a baseball jersey, even in the winter, and the cool air gave me goosebumps. I managed to snatch the corner of the comforter and pull it back over my hips before Mack burst through the door. Since he felt like I did about snow, I was surprised when he put his cold, wet hands on my cheeks and said, "Come on!

Rise and shine!"

"Go away," I told him and tugged the comforter tighter around myself.

Mack put his hands on Tasha's face. She tried to get free of him, but she was laughing. I propped my head on my hand and watched. I had managed to ignore their little interchanges until this point, but watching them play made me realize that I was ignoring the obvious.

Mack finally got tired and left Tasha and me alone. "What's up with you two?" I asked her.

"What do you mean?" she asked. She combed her hair back with her fingers and reached for a new fashion magazine on my bedside stand.

"Come on, Tasha. I do have eyes."

Tasha shut the magazine and studied me for a minute. "Okay. I like him. I have forever. He's sweet and smart and hot."

I put my hands over my face, gagging. "He's so not hot."

Tasha's got a quick temper. I could tell she was trying to be patient with me. "You shouldn't say that, Miranda—you guys are practically twins."

"So you really like him? Are you kissing and stuff?"

Tasha rolled her eyes. "I'm not going to answer that. I wanted to tell you, but it's not like you're around much these days."

She had me there. I sat up and leaned against the pillow, hugging my knees under the comforter. "Does anyone else know?"

"Just Carly. She's been working at Denny's, and Mack and I've been studying there."

"I know, too," Mom said, coming in through the door Mack had left open. She smiled at Tasha and sat on the edge of my bed.

"You do?" Tasha said. "How?"

Mom laughed. "Magical powers, I guess."

Tasha shook her head, then changed the subject by asking me, "So how's Keith?"

I glanced at Mom. I wanted to tell Tasha about the birth control conversation I'd had with him. I figured she'd be impressed with one of my choices for once. Maybe being with Mack would change how she felt about that stuff. But there's no way I'd talk about that in front of Mom, so I just said, "He's fine. He's coming over tonight to watch movies." Watching movies at home wasn't my idea of an ideal date, but Halloween in Boulder can be kind of wild, and Mom and Dad didn't let us go roaming around town. "You and Mack want to watch with us?"

Mack rapped on the open door before she could answer. "Dad made chili and it smells great. And Keith is on the phone."

I had turned off the ringer on my extension so it wouldn't wake me.

"Hey, Tash," Mack said. "Dad's going to take pictures of the snow family. He told me to get you. Come on."

I rolled my eyes, but she stood up giving me a wink.

I smiled back and reached for my phone, even though Mom stayed where she was. "Hi Keith."

"Hi, baby," he said. "Mack said you're still in bed. Are you sick?"

"No, just lazy. What's up?"

"My sister showed up last night."

"Really? She's about a month early." Jody hadn't gone back to college after she was raped, and Keith had said she was still in Tennessee playing in pickup bands. She had promised to come home for Thanksgiving. I remembered the night he had told me about what had happened to her and how much he missed her.

He answered, "I think she's low on money. She's eaten almost all the food in the house and now she's asleep. But she's going to sing tonight at a coffeehouse in Denver with a girl she knows, and she told me I could sit in on a few songs. Do you want to do that instead of the movies?"

"Sure. I want to meet your sister." That was true. I was curious to meet her, but I felt a little nervous, too. She seemed to have a big influence on Keith.

Keith hesitated and then said, "Do you think your parents will let you stay out later?"

I glanced at Mom. She had picked up the magazine Tasha left on the floor and was looking at the table of contents. My curfew was 11:30. Keith didn't have to be home till midnight. "Maybe. How late are we talking?"

"Jody is going to play till midnight as long as there's an audience."

"I'll ask, but if I can't, you should go without me." I didn't want him to miss the chance to sing.

"No, I don't want to go if you can't. We'll just get movies like we planned. I can sing some other time."

We could get movies anytime, but I said, "Okay—well, I'll ask and call you back."

"Ask what?" Mom said, when I hung up.

"Keith's sister is home from Nashville. She's a musician. She's playing tonight at a coffeehouse in Denver. Keith asked me if I wanted to go. Is that all right?"

Mom looked at the window and then back at me. "The roads aren't very good for driving late at night, Miranda."

I knew this wasn't going to be easy and I hadn't even asked about the curfew yet. "I know, Mom, but Keith will drive his new truck. You've seen it—it has a four-wheel drive with big tires. Keith named it Samson; it can get through anything."

Mom smiled. "I can tell you're going to have all the arguments worked out. How old is Keith's sister?"

"Around twenty, I think." The aroma of homemade chili was wafting through the house. I could hear my stomach making rumbling noises. I was suddenly starving.

"So it's definitely a coffeehouse? No alcohol?"

I nodded. Alcohol had never once come up since I'd been with Keith. I didn't think he ever drank anything. Ryan always took me to parties where the entire point was getting blasted. I'd had beer and rum and Coke, but I'd never been drunk. First of all, I didn't

really like the taste, and I knew if Dad and Mom thought I had been
drinking, I'd never be allowed out of the house again. "Keith is
going to sing with his sister. He's really amazing, Mom."

"How late?"

"Jody's playing till midnight. We'll be home after that. "

Mom touched my arm and stood up. "Let me talk to your dad
about it. I'll let you know. " That was a good sign. If she was going
to say no, she would have already said it.

After lunch, Mack and Tasha and I watched movies in the den
with cups of cocoa and the fireplace crackling. Tasha shared her
blanket with Mack, and neither of them made their usual jokes
during the romantic scenes. I knew Keith was waiting for me to call,
but I didn't want to rush my parents, so I just sat there with my
fingers crossed. Finally, Mom and Dad joined us in the den. Dad sat
on the loveseat with me and Mom took the rocking chair. She had
Josiah in her arms; he was sucking his thumb. When he was running
around with Ali he looked like a regular little kid, but cradled in
Mom's arms I remembered he was hardly more than a baby.

"I'll take him." Tasha said.

"No, I've got him," Mom said. "I'm not completely out of
practice."

"Where's Ali?" I asked.

"Coloring in the kitchen," Dad told me. A few minutes passed,
and when everyone was back into the movie, Dad slipped me his cell
phone. "One o'clock. Call if the roads are bad."

I was thrilled. But I just said, "Thanks, Dad."

Keith brought Jody in the house to meet my family when he
picked me up. She was thin— the kind of thin that comes from late
nights and skipping meals—but had the same white-blonde hair and
blue eyes as Keith had. She smiled at Mom and Dad, and I noticed
right away that she didn't have dimples and her eyes didn't sparkle
the way his did.

When Jody shook my hand, I could tell that she was looking me over just as closely as I was checking her out. I had had a hard time choosing what to wear and had gone casual—faded jeans that fit well, a royal blue sweater, and brown boots. Mom had let me take her leather bomber jacket—which was cool beyond words. I'd never been allowed to wear it before. But I could tell Jody was looking beyond what I was wearing.

Keith seemed as relaxed as ever. He waved to Mack, held the door open for Jody and me to go out first and promised Dad he'd drive carefully and have me home on time. But I felt more nervous than I ever had on a date. I was glad when he put his arm around me on the way to the truck. "You look nice," he said.

The snow had stopped and the plows had cleared the highway. We passed cars that had gone off the road during the storm and were waiting to be rescued from the drifts.

"So, Miranda," Jody said, reaching over me and turning the radio down, "have you heard my brother sing yet?"

I glanced at him. He was driving with both hands on the wheel. "Yeah, a few times."

"What do you think? Will he embarrass me?"

I smiled. "Not if you play loud enough."

Jody laughed.

Keith took his right hand from the steering wheel and squeezed my leg. "Hey, now. No being mean to the driver."

"I'm just kidding." I put my hand on top of Keith's but looked at Jody. "I'm sorry I have to be home at one."

"No problem. My parents would never have let me stay out past midnight when I was sixteen."

"You would have anyway," Keith reminded her.

"Shh," she hissed, looking around me at Keith. "I'm trying to make a good impression here."

I laughed. I didn't realize she would have any reason to be nervous about meeting me. It helped me relax a little. I could see why Keith missed her so much.

The coffeehouse was within walking distance of the University of Denver campus, but the crowd was diverse. College kids in expensive ski sweaters, people around my parents' age in jeans and turtlenecks, and a couple of old guys with beards and glasses playing chess in the corner. Most of the tables were full and the menu was written on a chalkboard. The special was hot cinnamon apple cider. Jody's friend was setting up a mike. Keith leaned his guitar against the wall and gave me a smile.

"Nervous?" I asked.

"A little. Want something to drink?"

Just then Jody waved us over and introduced us to her friend, Anna, who had dark skin and curly black hair. Anna told us we could order whatever we wanted and to say that we were with her. We went over to the counter to get drinks; Jody joined us.

"We're only going to play for about an hour or so. Until about nine or ten. If I'd known that, I wouldn't have dragged you guys down here."

"It's all right," Keith told her.

"Yeah, it's cool," I echoed.

She smiled. "Well, at least we won't have to worry about you being late, Miranda."

Keith had told me that Jody had received a full scholarship from the university, based on her classical violin performances, but I could see why she was finding work in Nashville. Her fingers flew on the fiddle strings, and when she put it down to join Anna at the mike, the entire coffeehouse was silent. Her voice was amazing. Wild applause broke out when she finished. Jody smiled and took the mike out of the holder.

"Thanks. I'd like you to welcome my brother, Keith. He prides himself on being a rock and roll street singer. Tonight he's making his debut as a bluegrass coffeehouse boy."

Keith squeezed my shoulder when he got up and gave me a

quick kiss on the cheek.

"Good luck, babe," I whispered, But he didn't need it. On the street his voice attracted attention even though he was singing over the noise of passing pedestrians, hot dog vendors, and traffic. Without those distractions, he completely captivated the audience; his voice gave me goosebumps. The crowd clapped and yelled for more when he was finished. But he took the mike as Jody had done and said, "Thank you. That's all my sister will let me play. She's afraid I'm going to upstage her."

Jody laughed and took the mike back. "I knew this would go to his head." The audience laughed, and Keith made his way back to me.

They finished up at about nine-thirty. Jody came over to us and said, "Anna invited us over to her place. Are you guys interested?"

Keith shrugged and looked at me.

"Sure," I said. Pale flakes were falling like confetti when we left the cozy, warm coffeehouse. Keith took my hand, and we followed Jody into the sparkling white night. The snow seemed magical.

fourteen

Driving to Anna's condo through the slick white streets, it occurred to me that my parents would want me to call if there was a change in plans, but I figured there were some things they were better off not knowing. Plus, I didn't want them to change their minds about my curfew. I was having too much fun watching Keith be stage-struck. His dimples hadn't disappeared once since leaving the mike. And when we got out of the truck to follow Jody and Anna up the sidewalk, he slipped his arm around my shoulder.

"I'm so glad you were with me tonight. Are you having fun?"

"A lot," I answered. "You were amazing."

He stopped and gave me a long, lingering kiss.

"You guys can do that in the house," Jody called to us. "It's freezing out here." Mack would have teased us, but Jody didn't seem to mind our affection. I figured Mack's attitude might change as things developed with Tasha. I was starting to see some advantages to their relationship.

Anna gave us a quick tour of the three-story condo. I took note of the very nice home theater in the basement and of the hot tub on the patio. I wondered what it would be like to soak in the hot foam with snowflakes filtering down. I traded a glance with Keith and could tell he was wondering the same thing.

Three other women shared the condo with Anna, and they all hugged Jody and told her she was too skinny. Then they hung around the kitchen catching up. Keith and I sat cross-legged on the floor in the living room wrapped up in our own conversation.

"What's better?" I asked him. "Singing in the street or singing with a mike and back-up?"

He laughed. "On the street I like people stopping to listen because they want to, not because they're being polite. Tonight was really cool, though." He put his hand on my knee. "I liked you watching me."

"I always like watching you." I leaned over and gave him a quick kiss, then glanced toward the kitchen. The rooms were only separated by a counter, but no one was paying attention to us.

He smiled. "I wish we could be alone for a while."

"We could check out that hot tub," I winked.

On cue, Jody leaned on the counter and said, "Hey, we're going to get something to eat."

Keith and I looked at each other. "Would it be okay to stay here?" he asked.

Jody hesitated, but Anna looked over the counter and said, "It's okay with me if they want to hang out here."

One of the roommates chimed in, "Let them stay. To be young again. Remember when making out on the couch was the best thing ever?"

Someone else said, "I still think it's the best thing ever."

Everyone laughed and Anna said, "Keith, you're so grown up now. Remember when he used to be skinny and clomp around in those cowboy boots all the time? I'd never have guessed he'd be bringing a cute girl around."

Everyone laughed again except for Jody. I liked that she didn't make fun of us, too. She checked her watch. "We're going to a Mexican place. It might take a while, but I'll make sure we're back so you aren't late, Miranda."

I nodded. Keith was still bright red from Anna teasing him. As soon as the women were gone, I ruffled his hair. "Cowboy boots, huh?"

"Don't tease. Mack showed me your seventh-grade braces picture."

"He did not."

"Wanna make a bet?" Keith laughed and took me into his arms.

"Hey," I whispered. "Let's move to the couch."

Keith nodded. "You want me to turn off the lights?" he asked.

"Okay." I took off my shoes and lay back on the couch. The room was not completely dark.

"I left the stove light on," he said, snuggling in between the back of the couch and me. I turned toward him and slipped my hand underneath his sweater, resting on his smooth, warm chest.

"Your sister's cool."

"She puts on a good show. But don't believe it all. I'm really kind of worried about her." He played with the ends of my hair, curling the strands around his pinky.

I thought about the summer night when Keith told me about Jody's rape. I thought about Mike trapping me against my locker, his fleshy, sweaty fingers on my shoulder. "Does she ever talk about what happened to her?"

He took a deep breath. "Not with me, and I'm probably closer to her than anyone. But I know it changed her. Shut off her emotions or something. I wish I could help her."

I kissed his cheek, wishing that I could help him.

He took his finger from my hair and traced my bottom lip. "She asked me if we were sleeping together."

"What did you tell her?" I wondered if he had shared with her what he knew about my past. I wasn't sure I liked that.

"I told her we weren't there yet. She asked what we were waiting for, but then she said she didn't know why she was surprised because she could always count on me to be a good boy."

"You are a good boy," I said, letting my hand fall from his chest to his stomach, the heel of my hand resting on the top button of his jeans.

"You make me wish I wasn't." He traced my lip with his finger again.

"You don't have to be, you know." I kissed his finger without taking my eyes off his. Part of me wished that he would be a little reckless once in awhile. It was getting harder for me to match his sense of control. And there in the dark, on a cozy, comfy couch, I thought about Jody's question. I wasn't sure what we were waiting for either. But I was still surprised when, for the first time ever, he unbuttoned my jeans and laid his hand on my abdomen, his fingers just touching the lace of my underwear. "Okay?"

I put my hand over his. "It's okay. I want you to."

Even though his touch was light and I could feel my body warming to the sensations, I squirmed out from underneath his hand. "I have to go to the bathroom, baby."

He nodded and let me up.

In the bathroom I looked at myself in the mirror over the sink. I took a deep breath. Thirty minutes ago I'd been wondering what we were waiting for, and all of a sudden I didn't know what I was thinking. I opened the drawer next to the sink to see if there were any condoms. Just in case. There was a brush and some yellow hair ties, nail scissors, a file, a bottle of bubblegum-pink nail polish, and a few loose tampons. I'd just finished my period a few days before, we'd probably be okay. I'd never take that chance though. What if Jody came back? I ran the brush through my hair. Was it worth the risk?

Keith was lying on his side, his head propped up on his hand. He had thrown the blanket that we had found in the hall closet over the back of the couch. I got settled back on the couch next to him, kissing his shoulder. His sweater was off; his skin was like a furnace. "Maybe we should stop, baby," he whispered, laying his hand on my stomach.

"Yeah. I'm scared your sister's going to come back."

He shook his head. "I think we have an hour. But I don't have any condoms."

I bit my lip. "I looked for some in the bathroom. You won't be upset if we wait then?"

Keith brushed my hair back from my face. "Of course not. I'm good with kissing."

I was, too, for about fifteen minutes. Then I pulled my sweater off and lay on top of him. He raked his fingers down my back and underneath the waist band of my jeans, but he whispered, "This is crazy, Miranda."

"I just finished my period. We'd be okay if you want to keep going." Even though the words came out of my mouth, I couldn't quite believe I said them.

He slid my bra straps off my arms, his hands warm and gentle on my skin, and whispered, "Are you sure?"

I nodded. I didn't bother taking one last listen for footsteps crunching in the snow on the walk. Instead I closed my eyes and told myself we'd be fine.

I'd always thought that drifting off to sleep after sex was just in movies. With Ryan, I'd always just gotten up and gone back to the party or rushed home before my curfew, totally wide awake and alert. And while I didn't fall asleep with Keith either, I faded into a dreamy state—totally relaxed and at peace—with my head cradled on Keith's shoulder. I was on my way to closing my eyes and completely forgetting where I was when the tune on Dad's cell phone made me jump.

I wriggled out from under Keith's arm and crossed the dark room to my jacket. I could see the clock on the microwave. 11:26.

"Hello?" I said, hoping I sounded awake.

It was Mom. "Hi. Are you leaving soon? It's really snowing here again."

"Yeah. Soon." Keith sat up too. He gave me a sleepy smile, and I wrapped my free arm over my chest and moved away from the dim light of the kitchen. After being tangled together under the blanket, I wasn't sure where my sudden modesty was coming from, but I realized that I felt a little vulnerable. Keith and I'd just stepped over a line changing our kisses and touches into something more adult and new. There was no going back.

"Call us if the roads are really icy."

"Okay, Mom." I didn't know how that would be helpful, but I kept the sarcasm out of my voice. I was a little annoyed that she was checking up on me, but too panicked about Jody's return to think about it much. I clicked the phone off.

Keith held out his hand to me. I didn't take it though, and instead, I reached for my jeans. "I'd die if your sister saw us like this."

Keith sat up. "You're right." Jody and her friends still weren't back even after we dressed and put the blanket back where it belonged. Keith held his hand out again. "Come here a minute."

I was still worried that Jody would be able to tell somehow, and I was really worried about that period thing. For the life of me I couldn't believe I'd been that stupid, but when I looked at Keith, I realized that he was asking to hold me. I flashed on my first time with Ryan. While he hadn't rushed into his clothes, he hadn't held me or asked me if I was okay, either. I'd wanted so much to cuddle, but had been too insecure to ask. Or maybe deep down I knew Ryan would have laughed at me.

For a minute I tried to forget about my worries, and walked across the room to Keith. "How are you, baby?" I asked him, slipping onto his lap and kissing his cheek.

"I'm okay," he answered. "That was really intense."

"It was. Were you nervous?"

"A little. Could you tell?"

I shook my head. "Not at all. You were great."

He smiled and kissed me, then met my eyes. "It was kind of dumb though. What if—"

He didn't have time to finish because the door flew open, letting in a blast of cold wind. "You guys ready to go?" Jody asked.

Keith's question wasn't finished, but I knew what he meant. It was dumb. And driving back on the slippery white highway with Keith's thigh touching mine and Jody singing softly along with the radio, I did the math again in my head. With his hands on my bare skin, it seemed like I just had my period. Now that I was thinking clearly, I realized the last day was Monday, nearly a week ago. I glanced at Keith in the dark. I was probably still safe. And it was only once. Maybe if Jody hadn't been with us, I would've told Keith what I was thinking, but I didn't. He trusted me. I lay my head on his shoulder and watched the big, white flakes swirl in the glow of the headlights as we drove into the storm.

fifteen

I woke with the memory of Keith's mouth on mine, his hands in my hair. I kept my eyes closed, trying to stay in the dream for as long as possible. I wondered what it would be like to sleep next to him all night and wake up together on a snowy morning snuggled under a warm comforter. I wasn't in any hurry to let go of that thought, but the pregnancy question stabbed into my head, making me get up and take down my calendar from the wall. Since I was twelve and had my first period, I'd kept track of the first day by putting a star by the date. I looked back through the year. I noticed that when I'd been on birth control, my cycles were more regular than they had been since going off in May. In fact there was no consistent pattern at all since then—three weeks to five weeks. The November dates were blank except for the red exclamation marks I'd written over the days of Thanksgiving break. I decided that if I didn't have my period by then, I'd be worried. Ironically, I was supposed to visit the clinic around that time. I wondered whether I should call and ask about the morning-after pill. I had always thought that pill was more for rape, not reckless behavior.

The phone rang, interrupting my thoughts. I answered my extension before the second ring. It was Keith. "Hey," he said. "How are you?"

"Fine." I told him. I didn't want to scare him about how I was really feeling; after all, I was the one that encouraged him in the first place. "How are you?"

"Good, but I want to see you. Hold you. Is that a possibility?"

"Probably." Sunday was family day, and we had to hang out together. But Keith and Tasha were mostly included as family. The tricky part would be getting time alone. "You want to come over about noon?"

"Okay."

I didn't want to leave my room and face Mom. Since I'd gotten home so late, no one really quizzed me over the events of the evening. I wasn't quite ready to lie about it, but hunger drove me downstairs. Mack was alone in the kitchen reading the paper. I put a large bowl of chili in the microwave.

He raised his eyebrows. "Chili for breakfast? Want me to make you some eggs to go with it?"

I nodded. Mack liked to cook but didn't usually offer. I knew that was a thanks for being cool about the new Tasha thing. I sat down at the counter and watched him get the eggs out of the refrigerator. He took out a tomato and some cheese. Excellent. Omelets.

"Where is everyone?"

He pointed to a piece of paper stuck to the bulletin board.

Mack and Miranda.

Went to breakfast.

Thought you would appreciate the extra sleep.

Don't go anywhere.

Mom, Dad and Ali.

"Did they say anything to you yesterday about what we were doing today?" I asked. I tried to be as casual as possible and keep the fact that I had an agenda out of my voice.

Mack wasn't fooled. "I think you're in luck. Mom said something about going into the office and working on some grading. Tasha and I might go ice-skating." There was a rink on campus that we could go to with Mom's faculty membership. Ali loved it. "Do you and Keith want to go?"

"Maybe." I didn't want Mack to think we didn't want to hang out with him, but I wasn't sure ice-skating would give me much chance to be alone with Keith. That's what I really wanted. Again I just wished that I could've spent the whole night with him.

I watched my brother use the edge of the knife to sweep the diced tomatoes into the skillet.

He noticed me watching him and smiled. "Did you have fun last night?"

I nodded. I didn't trust my voice on that answer, but I asked, "What did you guys do last night?"

"Do you want the chili on the side or over?"

"Over."

He spooned the chili over the eggs, then slid the plate across the counter. "We played Scrabble with Mom and Dad."

I refrained from rolling my eyes.

Mack laughed anyway. "I know what you're thinking, Miranda. You're not the only one who needs some time to get used to the idea. Dad almost fell out of his chair when he saw us holding hands."

I wasn't used to my brother being so serious, but I didn't tease. "Mom wasn't that surprised. She seems fine with it. A lot finer than she acts about Keith and me."

Mack noticed my resentment. "I think she worries about you and Keith spending so much time alone together. I think she thinks if Tasha and I are together, we'll all hang out more. It wouldn't be a bad idea."

I didn't say anything. I knew that Mom preferred that Keith and I do things with other people. Probably the only reason she'd let me go to Denver with Keith was that Jody was with us. I didn't realize it was so obvious to Mack though. But then he'd spent the last two months of school looking out for me. I got up and got myself a glass of water and looked out in the yard. The sun was bright and the snow was dripping from the railing of the deck and dropping in chunks from the bare tree branches. I turned to Mack. "I know what's been going on at school hasn't been easy for you. I'm sorry."

He met my eyes. "It's okay. It's been worse for you."

I returned to my stool and picked up my fork. "Keith isn't like Ryan, Mack."

"I know. I like Keith a lot, but he's still a guy, Miranda."

"You're a guy. Are you saying you'd treat Tasha like Ryan treated me?"

"Of course not. Just because I'm a nice guy doesn't mean I wouldn't do something stupid."

"This conversation is stupid. Why are we having it?" I didn't like how close Mack was to what had been bothering me all morning.

Mack shrugged. "I guess I'm just looking out for you. I don't want you to do anything you regret." At least he didn't say "again."

I took my plate to the sink and rinsed it off, then turned to Mack. "I do know what I'm doing, Mack. Really. I'll be fine."

Getting out of family day was just wishful thinking on Mack's part. Dad thought ice-skating was a great idea, and we all packed into Mom's minivan. Tasha and Mack got in the middle row, which left the back to Keith and me with Ali squirming her way between us. Again I wished for a family where parents didn't take such an active interest in my life.

After dropping Mom at her office, Dad parked over by the recreation center. Keith and I walked hand in hand over to the student union. It was the first time we'd really been alone together since rushing to put on our clothes the night before, and for once I felt shy. I didn't know how to even start telling him that I was worried. I wondered if he was.

The student union was a place I'd been to a hundred times with Mom. I loved to eat in the food court and watch movies in the small theater, but I'd never been back in the game room until I met Keith. There was a long room of pool tables with benches built into the wall, a small bowling alley, and a bunch of arcade games. Sunday was less crowded than after school, but music still rocked over the loudspeakers. We chose a pool table in the back of the room far away from the door. I watched Keith take aim for the break, concentrating, his muscles tense. He glanced up at me and his face broke into one of those smiles that captivated me. I smiled back and he took aim again, the muscles in his arms flexing. I thought about the way his muscles felt against my skin when held me close.

I whistled just as he hit the cue ball; it glanced the tip of the pyramid and barely scattered the balls.

Keith said, "No interference. I should get a rebreak."

"I don't think so," I told him, walking around the table looking for a shot.

He waited until I got set, then moved behind me and put his arms around my waist, kissing my neck. I missed by a mile. I laughed, "Okay, we're even now."

Keith laughed too but didn't let me go. I turned in his arms to face him. "Are you mad at me, baby?" he asked.

"Why?" I didn't know why I would be mad at him. If anything it should be the other way around.

He shrugged but didn't take his arms from my waist. "Last night. It was a lot more reckless than I wanted our first time to be. I guess I'm a little surprised that I let it happen that way. I had all these ideas that I'd be responsible and careful."

I bit the inside of my cheek. "Are you sorry?" Even I could hear the hesitation in my voice, I wasn't sure I wanted to hear his answer. I might be sorry that I was impetuous, but I wasn't sorry about being with him. I didn't want him to be sorry either.

"No. It was great. I love you." He leaned his forehead down on mine for a second, then met my eyes with his piercing blue eyes. "I just don't think I could handle you being pregnant."

I was squirming on the inside and surprised that my voice sounded so reassuring when I said, "We don't need to worry about that. It was a safe time. Being pregnant is the very last thing I want." The last part was true at least. I couldn't even imagine how I'd deal with that.

He held my face in his hands, letting the pool cue clatter on the linoleum. "Next time, we'll be careful."

I met his kiss without hesitation. Next time we would be.

While I half convinced myself that I was fine, I couldn't really keep my mind on the game. When Keith asked, "Want to take a walk?" I was only too glad to leave the loud reggae music and bright lights over the green tables for the Sunday silence of the campus.

We sat on the steps by the empty fountain, our thighs touching. Maybe because the night before had been so intense, for once just sitting together seemed fine. The winter sunshine warmed our faces and melted the snow around us.

"Know something, Miranda?" Keith asked me. "I've been thinking about what I'm going to be doing in the fall."

"Yeah?" I turned my head to look at him. I'd been trying to ignore the fact that he'd be applying to colleges soon. I was hoping he'd decide to stay in Boulder for school; I couldn't stand the thought of him going away. When Ryan had applied for college, I'd felt relieved. An end in sight without an ugly breakup.

"My parents still want me to go to an agricultural program." He shrugged. "But I always do what they want me to do. Seems like my whole life I've been the good boy while Jody does whatever she wants."

"What do you want to do?" I asked, almost holding my breath.

"That's the thing. I probably do want to be on the ranch one day, but I don't see how an agricultural program will help me do something I've been doing my whole life. I guess I want to go to college, but I could stay here and take some businesses classes or some music classes." He looked at me. "Have you thought about what you're going to do for college?"

"Not much." Tasha and Mack talked about college all the time, but I felt sort of like Keith. I knew I wanted to do something in art, but I wasn't sure how college would help me with that. I really didn't want to think that far ahead. And I didn't want to think about being away from Keith at all.

He seemed to read my mind. "I just want to be near you."

"Me too." I settled my head back against his body, still thinking about my period. If I was pregnant, I wondered if he'd be so eager to stay. I pushed that thought away, too. There was just no way that life could be that unfair.

sixteen

My period came a week and a half later during English while I was finishing up a short-answer test. I could feel the subtle dampness and a twinge of a cramp across my back. Mrs. McDonald didn't like us leaving the room during tests, but she didn't object when I picked up the hall pass and slipped from the room. I kept tampons in my locker... but was carrying one around in my pocket, thinking that it might inspire my body to do what I wanted. There were only a few drops of blood in my underwear, but that's all I needed to breathe a sigh of relief.

When I came out of the stall, I went to the window. The bathroom overlooked the street where Keith always waited for me. He got out of school earlier than I did, so I checked to see if he was waiting. He wasn't, which was probably a good thing because I was so thrilled about starting my period, I might have just walked right out of school. Instead I took a deep breath and washed my hands at the sink. The queasy, nervous feeling I'd been carrying around disappeared. It was the first time I'd relaxed since that coffeehouse night.

Mrs. McDonald handed back some essays we'd written on Mary Shelley's *Frankenstein* just seconds before our release. Except for mine. The policy was that if a paper wasn't handed back, you had to wait. I considered just escaping with the rest of the class, but Mrs. McDonald was too smart for that. She stood near the door. A bad grade on an English paper wasn't that big a deal to me, considering I'd spent the last week and a half stressing out about my life being ruined. But I knew my teacher wasn't going to see it that way.

When Mrs. McDonald handed me my essay, I folded it in half

and shoved it into my notebook. "I'm in a hurry, Mrs. McDonald. Someone is waiting for me."

"I think being in a hurry was part of your problem on the essay, Miranda. And besides, it's not like Mr. Motorcycle's going anywhere." I blushed, realizing that teachers had more of a clue than they let on. I wondered what else Mrs. McDonald observed. She said, "Let's take a look at the essay," and I sat down.

The essay was covered in red and didn't have a letter grade at the top. "Truth. How long did you spend on this?" she asked me.

"Not long," I admitted. The essay was assigned over the coffeehouse weekend, and I just didn't have time to think about things like books. Instead, I scribbled out a page in math the day it was due. I got away with stuff like that on my history essays, but Mrs. McDonald knew better. Even though my punctuation wasn't always perfect, I usually had original ideas and didn't just sum up the book like I know a lot of people do.

"Not long is evident. You can rewrite it for a higher grade."

I looked at the essay. "Well, what grade is this?" I had an "A" in English. I figured one bad grade wouldn't kill my average, but I had to have decent grades or Mom and Dad would make me come right home after school instead of letting me spend time with Keith.

Mrs. McDonald didn't appreciate my carefree attitude. "I see your mother at the gym sometimes, Miranda. I'm sure she would have something to say about this."

I was sure she would, too. I raised my eyebrows at Mrs. McDonald. She had never resorted to blackmail before, but I'd never given her reason to, either. And she could've called Mom without giving me a chance. Or just given me the grade I deserved. I met my teacher's eyes. "When do you need it?"

"Monday."

That was more than fair. "Okay," I said, folding the essay more carefully this time.

She nodded, but she didn't seem ready to let me go. "You've seemed a little distracted lately. Anything I can help with?"

I shook my head. "I'm fine." That was the truth now.

Mrs. McDonald studied me for a minute, probably to see if I was going to change my mind about sharing, but then she stood up, "I guess you shouldn't keep Motorcycle Boy waiting any longer."

I stood up and laughed. "His name's Keith." Shifting my books to my hip, I said, "Thanks for being cool about the essay."

She flashed me a smile. "Don't let me down."

I didn't bolt down the hall like I normally did. I was feeling kind of tired and crampy. My period didn't usually affect me like that. Walking across the dead winter lawn I wondered how to tell Keith and be calm about it at the same time. He still didn't know how freaked out I'd been.

Keith was waiting for me in the truck and listening to the radio. "Hi," he said, leaning over and kissing my cheek. "Did you get in trouble?"

"Yep. I have to rewrite an English assignment. How did you know?"

"You're usually one of the first people out of the building." He pulled into traffic. The street was one way and led away from my house.

I slid close to him, and he put his hand on my thigh. "You want to hang out at my house?" I asked him. Ali had Brownies on Wednesdays, and it was Mom's turn to help out with the troop. Since Mack had his new thing with Tasha, he didn't always come straight home. But for once I wasn't thinking about a way to be alone. All I wanted to do was lie on the couch for a while. And maybe take a nap. I put my head on Keith's shoulder.

"Are you all right?" Keith asked.

I hoped the relief wasn't evident in my voice when I said, "I have my period and I'm sort of achy."

He squeezed my hand. "I'm sorry, but the period part is good, right?"

I tilted my head so I could see his profile. "You were worried?"

He glanced at me and took a deep breath before saying, "A little. I know you said it was a safe time, but what if it wasn't? Did you think about how we'd handle that?"

"Some," I admitted. "Mostly I hoped I wasn't wrong about the safe thing. I didn't want you to be mad."

He squeezed my hand again. "I wouldn't be mad. I was there too, remember? But I'm glad we don't have to worry about it anymore."

I was glad, too, and more than I let on.

The house was cold. Dad insisted on keeping the heat turned down during the day. Keith and I snuggled under a fleece blanket in the den, and after a few minutes of cartoons I was asleep with my cheek against his chest. I didn't wake up until Ali shouted, "Miranda and Keith are sleeping together on the couch!"

Keith and I both opened our eyes. "What did she just say?" Keith asked. Ali was standing over us, grinning, with face paint covering her cheeks and forehead.

I glared at my sister, "Go away." I didn't bother separating myself from Keith. We weren't doing anything wrong, and I was still tired. I closed my eyes again.

"Ali, wash up," Mom said, coming into the den. Keith struggled to sit up, so I made an effort also, but I really just wanted to go back to sleep. When Ali was out of earshot, Mom asked, "What's going on?" I noticed that face paint had attacked Mom too. She had daisies or something like them on her cheeks.

"We fell asleep, I guess," Keith told her, rubbing his eyes. "Miranda isn't feeling that well."

I leaned back against the couch. "We weren't doing anything, Mom."

Keith blushed, but Mom came over to me and put her hand on my forehead. "I see that, Miranda. What's wrong?"

I didn't push her hand away, but I didn't like being treated like a baby in front of Keith. "I'm fine. Just tired."

"You're not warm, but maybe you're coming down with something."

"I'm fine," I said again. "I'll go to bed early tonight."

Keith didn't stand up, but he did say, "Maybe I ought to go home so you can rest."

I didn't want him to leave, but I was really wiped out. I smiled at him and put my hand on his thigh. "Sorry I'm such a drag today."

He squeezed my hand and gave me a kiss on the forehead, even though Mom was still there. "It's okay, baby. I'll call you later and see how you are."

I expected Mom to lay into me about bringing Keith to an empty house, but she just put the blanket back over me and sat down on the edge of the couch. "I'm sorry you're not feeling well, but I'm glad that's what I walked into. When Ali said you and Keith were sleeping together, all sorts of things went through my head."

I gave her a weak smile and lay back down on the couch. "I'm sort of queasy. I started my period today."

Mom looked concerned. "You don't usually get cramps, do you?"

I shook my head. "This is the first time."

She put her hand on my forehead again, and this time I didn't mind. Her fingers were cool and smooth and made me think of when I was small and sick and she'd hold me and whisper stories. I closed my eyes. "Do you get cramps, Mom?"

"Sometimes. Do you want me to get you something for them?"

I didn't want her to leave, so I shook my head and said, "Would you give me a back rub, please?"

"Okay. Turn over." She gave great back rubs, but they were rare treats. When Keith gave me back rubs, my whole body sizzled, but when Mom touched my skin it was like sinking into warm sand.

"You've lost weight. How come?"

"Don't know," I answered, although I was aware that I had dropped a few pounds. Worrying affected my appetite. I was on the thin side, so even a little weight loss was noticeable. "School's been kind of hard lately." At least that was sort of true, I rationalized, thinking of my English essay.

"Anything I can help with?"

I shrugged, glad that she couldn't see my face too clearly. "I don't think so."

She rubbed my shoulders, then my neck. I closed my eyes.

"Miranda?" Her voice was hesitant and I opened my eyes again. "Yeah?"

"I know you and Keith were just sleeping today, but you looked awfully comfortable together on the couch."

It wasn't a question, but I knew Mom hoped for an answer. I considered what to say, finally opting for, "Yeah, I guess we probably did."

She didn't move her hands from my shoulders, but her voice had some hesitation in it when she asked, "How's that choice thing going for you?"

I closed my eyes, glad that she couldn't read the expression on my face. I couldn't lie to her, but I couldn't tell her the truth either. I answered her question with a question. "Mom, can I ask you something?" I twisted over and laced my fingers behind my head.

She put her hands in her lap and nodded.

"How long did you wait with Dad?" I'd never been brave enough before to ask Mom about her sex life, but I was interested.

"Your father and I were almost finished with college when we met."

"So does that mean you're not going to tell me?" It didn't seem fair that she could expect me to answer her questions and avoid mine.

She looked at the TV screen and then back at me. I could tell that she was debating how much to tell me. "About two months, maybe a little less." She sighed. "If I'd known my daughter was going to be asking me one day, I would've waited longer." Tears surfaced in her eyes, confusing me. What exactly was she sad about?

I sat up, wanting to touch Mom or something, but I didn't and I didn't know what to say. I always thought my mom did everything right. It was hard for me to believe that she made mistakes or got swept away.

"But you love Dad, right?" I could hear the hesitation in my voice. If she didn't love him, did I want to know that?

Mom looked at me quickly and wiped her cheeks. "Of course I love your dad. But looking back, I'm not sure why we were in such a hurry. We could have enjoyed each other more without complicating things so soon in our relationship."

I knew what she meant about complicating things, but even so, I didn't know how I could change things now. "But it worked out for you and Dad."

"Yes, but it's not always sunlight and kisses." Mom pushed her hair back from her forehead and then let it fall through her fingers. She studied me like she was trying to figure out what to say next. "Have you already been with Keith?"

"One time. It just sort of happened." I didn't see any point in lying about it, but even so I could feel the blush spreading across my face. The specifics of my recklessness would just kill Mom.

She took a deep breath. "Okay then. I guess I'm not going to be able to talk you into waiting a while longer." She looked at the TV screen for a minute then back at me. "What about birth control? Do you need me to make an appointment for you?"

"I'm good on that," I told her, feeling guilty that I could dare to say that. "Mom, I do love him."

"I know you do, Miranda." She put her hand on my leg. "This is going to be hard for me, honey. I'm not mad, but it's not something I can be happy about either." She gave my thigh a light squeeze and left me alone.

There were still questions I wanted to ask her. I wondered if she had other regrets. I wondered if she had ever been on edge waiting for her period. She always said that she planned to have Mack and me close together, but maybe it wasn't such a plan. I always thought

I was pretty good about only telling Mom what I wanted her to know, but I never once considered there were two sides to that. I wondered if she had secrets like I did, but I was too drained to think about it much more. I dragged myself upstairs, changed tampons, and fell asleep on top of my comforter. When I woke hours later, the house was dark and I was starving. I made my way into the kitchen and ate a banana at the kitchen counter without turning on the light. Before going back to sleep, I went into my bathroom. The tampon box was almost empty, but it turned out that I didn't need one, because the tampon I pulled from my body was white and dry. The bleeding had stopped.

seventeen

I was up the rest of the night, checking every thirty minutes to see if I'd started bleeding again. I tried that power of positive thinking thing. Periods could be as short as one day and still count. I was sure I'd heard that in my health class in eighth grade. But what if it wasn't true? How would I tell Keith? How could I tell Mom when I'd already said I was good when she asked me about birth control? What would Tasha say? Would I ever be able to look at my father again?

I got down the calendar again and tried to average out the length of my periods over the last eleven months, still trying to hold on to the hope that even if a period lasted only for a few hours, I was still safe. Finally at five in the morning, I gave up trying to sleep and took a long hot shower. Then I slipped out of the house and walked over to Tasha's.

Frost laced the trees and there was just enough morning light for me to avoid the slippery spots on the sidewalks. I didn't know what to say to Tasha; she wouldn't be overwhelmingly sympathetic to my stupidity. But she was my best friend and she had never let me down before.

The light from Tasha's room was visible at the bottom of her door, but the shower was running in the bathroom. Carly called to me from her room, her door ajar. "Tasha just turned the water on. What's up?"

"I'm sorry, I didn't mean to wake you up," I told her, moving closer so I could keep my voice low and not wake Josiah. He was lying like a spoon against Carly. She had her arm over him so he wouldn't roll onto the floor. His toddler bed was across the room and neatly made.

"I wasn't asleep. The draft in this room is really bad in the winter and Josiah gets cold, but sleeping with him is killing me. I need to figure something else out."

The room was cold and I crossed my arms for warmth.

"Sit down," she whispered, waving to the rocking chair. "I haven't seen you in forever." She didn't sit up, but propped her head on her hand and pulled the blanket up higher on Josiah. He didn't budge.

"He's getting big," I said, wrapping up with the soft baby quilt draped across the back of the rocker.

"Mmm. He is. He sure loves Mack."

"Has Mack been hanging out here a lot?"

"Some. Were you just blown away by that? Tasha was terrified to tell you."

Not as terrified, I bet, as I was to tell her about the coffeehouse night, but I smiled and said, "I just think he's such a geek and don't get how anyone could possibly like him. Especially my best friend. I mean, she has taste."

Carly laughed. "She's also a lot smarter about guys than I am. And Mack looks pretty good in T-shirts and he's great with Josiah and he can cook. What more can you ask for? I'm thinking I might make a play for him myself if Tasha's not smart enough to hold on to him."

"Great, just pass my brother around. That's all he needs for his ego." The shower was still going. Tasha always used all the hot water in the morning because no one else got up until much later. I thought maybe I could talk to Carly about my problem. At least she had some experience and she wouldn't yell at me like Tasha would. "Carly, can I ask you something?"

"Sure. Thinking about running off to Mexico or something?"

I couldn't help smiling, but I shook my head. "Here's the deal, Carly. I think I skipped my period."

"You think?" She raised her eyebrows. "You either skipped it or you didn't."

"I know, but I started at school yesterday, and around midnight—nothing—it was all over. Could that be defined as skipped?"

Carly put her hand on Josiah's head, smoothing his curls. "Yeah. I think. Gosh, Miranda. You've been on birth control forever. What happened?"

"I went off in May when Ryan left. Keith and I were together for the first time a couple of weeks ago. We didn't use anything; I thought it was a safe time."

She studied me and for a second I thought she was going to lecture me, but said, "I've been there. You just don't think it'll happen. How do you feel?"

"Besides scared as hell? I've been tired for the last day or two."

"Like really sleepy tired?"

When I nodded, she asked. "Sore breasts?"

"A little. They feel heavier, but sometimes I feel that way before my period. I didn't think it was that unusual."

Josiah shifted and put his thumb in his mouth. Carly pulled the blanket up on his shoulder again. "I don't know, Miranda. Sounds like you need to take a test. You can get one from the grocery store. At least that way you'll know."

"Is that what you did?"

"Yep. After the test was over, I threw it on the floor and stomped on it. Didn't make me feel any better though."

I was quiet, thinking about Tasha telling me that Carly was pregnant. The boy was a University of Colorado freshman majoring in chemistry. He didn't come back to college after Christmas break that year. I remembered being sad for Carly but didn't really comprehend all the responsibility that was hitting her. I was comprehending it now. The shower was turned off and Carly and I looked at each other, but then the blow dryer started.

"Does Tasha know about you and Keith yet?"

I shook my head.

She leaned forward. "Don't tell her until you know for sure.

She'll freak."

"I'm freaking out myself."

"Yeah, I remember that feeling." She looked down at Josiah, then back up at me. "Take the test. If you're not pregnant, you can relax."

"Maybe I should go before Tasha comes out. She'll know something's wrong."

Carly nodded. "Let me know, okay? I'll do whatever you need me to do."

I slipped out the door and down the steps to the sidewalk. The sky was as light as it was going to get, a dim white gray. I folded my arms tight underneath my chest, feeling a stabbing tenderness for the first time. I remembered Carly's question about sore breasts, and hoped that it was just the power of suggestion. I hoped that I wouldn't have to ask her for anything else, but I was glad that I could count on her if I did.

When I got home, Mom was standing by the toaster, yawning, and Dad was squeezing orange juice. I could tell from the astonishment on their faces that they both thought I was still in my room. Dad recovered first. "Where have you been?"

"Just went over to Tasha's for a minute."

He stared at me like I'd lost my mind. "Is the phone broken? Why couldn't you call her?"

I felt like saying, "Do you really want to know, Dad?" Instead I said, "I just needed to see her without Mack around, which isn't so easy lately." I got myself a yogurt out of the fridge.

"Are you feeling better?" Mom asked.

I wasn't. The smell of the brewing coffee was making me nauseated, or maybe it was just my talk with Carly. But I said, "I'm fine."

Mom and Dad exchanged a look.

Dad said, "You aren't just saying that so you can see Keith later, are you?"

"Well, if I stay home can I hang out with him when he gets out of school?"

They exchanged that look again. This was obviously something that they discussed and come to a conclusion over ahead of time. Mom answered, "You can go one day without seeing him, Miranda."

I could go one day without seeing him, but I didn't want to, even if that meant that later I would be delivering the results of a pregnancy test. Before I could answer, the phone rang.

"Hi Miranda." It was Keith. "Feeling better?"

"Yeah." I told him. "I was just tired."

"That's what your Mom said when I called last night. She said you were sleeping."

I looked at Mom. She was chewing on her nails. She looked more tired than I felt. I wondered how much sleep she lost worrying about me. And she didn't even know how worried she should be.

"See you after school?" he asked.

"Okay." I wondered what kind of news I'd have for him by then.

Mom tilted her head and studied me when I hung up the phone. "You still look tired, honey. I think you should stay home."

"I'm fine, really." If I kept saying that, maybe it would be true.

I couldn't bring myself to buy a test right away. Even though Carly yelled at me and threatened to tell Tasha my secret, I decided to keep to my Thanksgiving break deadline, and if my period didn't start again by then, I'd get a pregnancy kit at the grocery store. Most of the time, though, all I kept thinking was *What if?*, over and over. I totally bombed an art history test. I couldn't concentrate on the essay questions and just turned them in blank. I spilled a bottle of red glaze all over the floor in my ceramics class, and I got to the point where I was checking to see if my period had restarted between every class. After a week of doing that, I couldn't take it anymore. I told Mack and Tasha during lunch that I needed to run home and grab my English essay, and borrowed the keys to the Jeep.

But I didn't go home.

I hadn't known there were so many pregnancy tests on the market, and I had no idea which would be best. After reading a couple of the packages, I just grabbed one in a blue box thinking about Keith's eyes. Maybe blue would bring me luck. Smuggling the test home was probably not the best option, so I paid for it and took the plastic bag into the store's bathroom.

The directions weren't complicated, but peeing on a tiny window was messier than I would have thought. The salty, tangy smell of the urine almost made me gag, and as soon as I laid the test stick on top of the toilet paper dispenser, I tore off some of the tissue and wiped my fingers. If a pink line appeared, my life was over. And so was Keith's. For the first time I thought about what this would do to him. I sat on the toilet with my head in my hands. I didn't want to look. If it was negative, I could just keep it a big secret and learn from the experience. I closed my eyes tight and promised I'd never do anything so stupid again.

But it was too late. Even though the line was pale, it was still there and definitely pink. I don't know how long I sat there on the toilet seat with my body folded over onto my lap, letting my tears soak into the denim of my jeans. For some reason, my mind flashed to my old copy of *Beauty and the Beast*. The color of pink on the pregnancy stick was the same pink as Belle's dress on the last page when the Beast becomes the handsome prince. So much for happy endings.

eighteen

Somehow I made it back to school, although I can't remember a single detail about leaving the store or driving. I considered going out to Keith's school, but I didn't have a clue what to tell him. And I guess I figured that I was in enough trouble without adding truancy to my problems. I was late, though, and the halls were empty. If it was any other class I would have just gone to algebra without stopping at my locker, but I needed my book in order to appear as normal as possible to Mack and Tasha. I was thinking so hard about the pink line and what that meant that I didn't notice Mike Jergens until I felt his heavy hand on my shoulder.

"Alone at last, sweetheart," he whispered in my ear.

I spun around to face him. He was grinning a stupid, triumphant grin as he put his hands on either side of me against the locker wall and said, "And I've heard all about what happens when a guy gets you alone."

The veins in his forearms were popping out and the muscles in his biceps didn't escape my attention, but I had bigger worries than his games. "You wish," I told him, trying to duck under his arm like I had when he trapped me before.

This time the hall wasn't packed with witnesses, and he grabbed my hair and yanked me back against my open locker door. His free hand slid down to my breast, and there was no ignoring the stabbing tenderness. Still grinning, he stepped closer and said, "Why are you running away, Miranda? I just want to talk to you."

He took his hand from my hair and stroked my cheek with his big, meaty forefinger, shifting his weight so that I was pressed against the metal locker door. I yelled and tried to wriggle free, but he slapped me and hissed, "Shut up," just inches from my face. The sharp smell of his sweat and coffee breath overpowered me. I gagged and then threw up. Mike jumped back, but not before vomit hit his chin and soaked his black fleece pullover.

Still gagging, I swiped at my mouth with the heel of my hand and met Mike's eyes, taking in his confusion and surprise. "That's what I think of you, loser."

I registered his shock transforming into rage, but I didn't have time to get out of the way before his fist caught the side of my face and knocked me for a second time against the metal locker.

The pain in my cheek was splintering, and I barely comprehended that the hall was suddenly swimming in people, among them Mack tearing into Mike. My brother wasn't a fighter, but that wasn't evident from all the punches he was landing. I tried to get to my feet, but a wave of nausea hit me again, and I slumped back against my locker.

Most school fights I'd seen were short—some circling and shoving, maybe a punch or two. This one was different; it took three big teachers to break it up, and then both boys had to be held back from each other. Mike was led away first. Then Mack's baseball coach tried to take Mack, but my brother shook off the hold and came to me. He knelt next to me and tilted my chin up so he could see my face, but I kept my hand against my cheek.

"Are you okay?" he asked me, getting blood all over my shirt.

I nodded, sure that my bruises were nothing compared to his. "I'm sorry, Mack."

"It's not your fault, Miranda. It's not your fault at all." Then he went with his coach.

But it was my fault. All of it. Tasha sat next to me and put her arm around me. "What happened, Miranda?" I didn't even know where to start, and if we had been alone I might have told her about my short period and the pregnancy test and the way the coffee smell made me sick, but instead I crumpled into sobs.

Since being punched in the face is worthy of uncontrollable

sobbing, no one even questioned that I might be upset about something more. I was conscious of voices discussing what to do for me, and someone—I think Tasha—suggested getting Mrs. McDonald.

Mrs. McDonald was all business, even though she crouched next to Tasha and her touch was gentle on my shoulder. "Miranda, you need to go to the nurse's. Can you walk?"

I nodded through my tears and took my hand from my cheek. When I tried to stand a second time, I stumbled against the lockers.

Tasha sucked in her breath and held my arm to help steady me. "He really got you this time."

"This time?" Mrs. McDonald asked. "There have been other times?"

I put my hand back up to my cheek. "I'm feeling sick again. Do you think we could move somewhere so I can lie down?" I wasn't avoiding the question; I just really didn't feel well at all.

They helped me to the nurse's office and led me to a tiny room with a bed. I lay down, choking back sobs, staring up at the ceiling, my hands folded against my stomach. I knew Tasha would tell Mrs. McDonald everything she knew about Mike pressuring me. Even though my cheek was throbbing, Mike didn't seem that important anymore. I was just thinking about Keith and what I was going to say to him. I closed my eyes and tried to shut out the lights and my thoughts and my pain.

The nurse shook my arm. "Hey, you've been hit in the head pretty hard, I don't want you sleeping."

I sat up and leaned against the wall, wishing sleep was even a possibility. She handed me an ice pack and watched me touch my cheek with it. It hurt too much for any pressure. "Hold it on the bruise, Miranda. It'll help with the swelling."

I nodded and put the pack back to my face, clenching my teeth as the cold and pain mingled together. Someone must have told the nurse my name. She was new to the school, and because I never used the nurse's office, I didn't pay much attention to remembering her name when she was introduced at the first school assembly.

"Good job," she told me. "Someone called your father. Both of your parents are coming. Are you ready to talk about what happened? Mrs. McDonald wants to ask you some questions."

I nodded, figuring there was no way out of it. Mrs. McDonald was missing class, but she was the kind of teacher who would see something like this through. She sat across from me and moved a strand of her dark hair behind her ear. She was about Mom's age and had a single gold band on her left hand. I knew nothing about her personal life. Sometimes she wore jeans, but today she had on khaki dress pants and a white polo shirt. Teacher clothes. "So I guess you've been dealing with a lot," she said, breaking the silence.

That was one way of looking at it, but she meant Mike. I shrugged. "It wasn't all that bad until today."

"What do you mean?"

"Well, mostly it was just talk. Names and stuff. He sometimes tried to touch me but never hurt me." I didn't want to get any more explicit than that. It was embarrassing enough and I was sure Tasha had filled her in on the details. "Today's the first time he wouldn't let me go."

"He's saying he hit you because you threw up on him."

"I did throw up on him," I said, almost gagging again at the flash of his mouth so near mine and the strong coffee smell. "He wouldn't let me go, and he makes me sick."

Mrs. McDonald gave me a small smile when I said that. "Well, that's one way of letting a boy know you're not interested." But she was serious again when she asked, "How come you never told anyone about this?"

I shrugged again. "I thought I could handle it."

She nodded, studying my face. I could tell she was thinking about what she was going to say to me next. Mrs. McDonald wasn't afraid of getting personal, but she said, "The school called the police and reported it as an assault. You don't have to handle it alone anymore."

That got my attention. "You mean I'm going to have to talk to the police? What about Mack? Is that assault, too?" My brother had never been in trouble in his life.

Mrs. McDonald shook her head. "Normally fistfights aren't reported as assaults unless there are extenuating circumstances. Mack was provoked to a certain extent. He'll probably be suspended for a day or so; that's just standard. I don't know for sure."

Tears spilled from my eyes; this was getting way out of hand. I dropped the ice pack and said, "Do you think you could get Tasha for me?" But we heard Dad's voice in the hall and then he was there, gathering me in his arms, holding me tight against his soft denim work shirt.

"Are you okay, baby?"

Mom stood in the entryway watching us. I thought about those times at night when she smoothed my hair back. I had thought about telling her about Mike, but I didn't want to worry her. I never once thought I'd have even bigger problems.

There was no way I even knew where to start. The sobs came rushing back. Mrs. McDonald left and Mom sat with Dad and me on the bed. "It's okay, honey," she told me.

It was so not okay, and it was a few minutes before I could get myself under control. I swallowed and pushed away from Dad's chest. "Is Mack okay? It's my fault if he's hurt."

Mom and Dad looked at each other, then Dad said, "We haven't seen him yet. On the phone they said his hand might be broken. Do you want to tell us what happened?"

I swallowed and looked at Mom. I didn't really want to tell my dad anything. Sooner or later the whole ugly saga was going to come out. Mom was going to catch on about how it all got started because she knew about Ryan, but Dad still thought of me as his baby. I wondered if he'd hold me as tightly when he knew the truth. Or if he'd hold me at all if he knew the whole truth about everything.

Mom put her hand on my arm. "You need to be able to talk about it, Miranda. The police are here, and we're pressing charges."

"Please, can we just let it go? I'm okay." I didn't have the energy for the police. I needed the questions to stop. "What about Mack? Aren't you going to check on him?"

Mom and Dad looked at each other again, then Dad let me go and stood up. "I'll check on Mack, but I'll be back."

Mom touched my sore check. "Why don't you want to say anything? He hurt you."

I put my head in my hands so I wouldn't have to look at Mom. "I just can't right now, Mom. Please just let me go home."

"Miranda, how long has this been going on?"

"I don't know. A while."

"You never told anyone? Not even Keith?"

I shook my head, but didn't look up from my hands. Keith had asked me if Ryan's friends were giving me a hard time after I told him about the first day of school, but I told him things were okay. I never thought Mike was going to attack me or hit me. Telling Keith wouldn't have helped anyway. He would have done the same thing Mack did.

Mom let out a deep breath and put her hand under my chin, making me look at her. "Ryan told his friends about you, didn't he?"

I was crying again.

"Look baby, Mike had no right to hit you or harass you." Her eyes were serious and her voice was low but firm. "You didn't deserve this. And you're going to have to talk to the police. He can't do this anymore."

"Does it have to be today? Can't I just go home? I'm sick." That was the absolute truth. Pulling away from Mom, I sobbed into my hands again.

"It's not going to take long, and we'll be with you."

I took my hands away from my face. "I can't do it in front of Dad." Talking to strangers about a boy's hands on me was going to be hard enough, but I couldn't do it with Dad watching. If I had to do it I wanted to do it by myself.

"Your Dad is going to hear some of what's happened, if not all of it, Miranda. There's no way around it now."

I pulled my hair up off my neck and held it on top of my head. I was still aching in the spot where Mike had yanked my hair. "But I can't talk about it in front of Dad. Please just let me talk to the police while he's with Mack."

Mom stood up and went out into the office. I lay on my side on the bed with my hands clamped between my knees. I closed my eyes, wondering how things got so messed up, so fast.

I don't know how much time passed while I was alone. It seemed like forever. I was still lying on my side when Dad came back and sat down on the edge of the bed next to me. "Miranda, Mack needs to go to the hospital. His hand is broken. Mom's going to be with you when the police interview you. They're waiting for you in the principal's office."

I sat up and combed my hair back from my face. Dad watched me, and I could tell there was something else he wanted to tell me, but he gave me a hug and said, "We'll talk when we get home."

Great. Something more to look forward to, but I took a deep breath and stood up with him.

I'd never been in the principal's office before for any reason. It was big, with nice blue carpeting and paintings of lakes and aspens on the walls. The police officer was a woman with brilliant red hair. Her nightstick jutted out when she sat down. Mom sat in a chair next to me. She was close enough to touch me, but she was looking down at her nails. For the hundredth time I noticed that we had the same hands, long and lean. But for the first time I realized I could be passing those hands on to a child. That was too much to think of and I tried to concentrate on what our principal was saying to me. Something about the school's responsibility in sexual harassment cases. I didn't hear half of it, but I nodded like I did. The street was visible out the principal's office window. School was almost over and Keith would be pulling up soon. I was both relieved and terrified.

The questions weren't too hard. A summary of the events in the hall. No background stuff. I didn't have to recount the day Mike first slid the tank top strap off my shoulder or the way my hands shook. The police officer took some Polaroids of me and set them down to develop in the swath of sunlight on the principal's smooth oak desktop. Shocked at the angry purple contusion emerging across my pale skin, I picked up one of the photos, putting my other hand against my cheek. Everyone went silent and I looked up from the picture to meet the police officer's warm brown eyes. She said, "You were lucky he didn't shatter your jaw."

Lucky. I never felt further from lucky in my life. I looked at Mom, the waterworks starting again. She touched my arm but looked at the principal, then the police officer. "May I take her now?"

I wanted to leave before the halls swarmed with noise, but I hung back on the steps leading out of the building. "Mom, Keith will be here soon. He won't know what happened."

Mom continued down the steps and looked back up at me. "Tasha said she'd tell him what's going on. Mack gave her the keys to the Jeep. She's going to get Ali and meet us at the hospital."

"The hospital? Why can't we wait for Mack at home?"

"Miranda, you need to be examined too."

"What?" I tried to control the panic in my voice. There was no way I was going to be examined by a doctor and be asked all sorts of personal questions in front of my mom today. "I'm fine. Really. It's just a couple of bruises. Just let me go home." I didn't think I could possibly cry any more, but I was wrong. I sank down on the steps. "Mom, I just can't."

She came back and sat next to me, putting her arm around me. "I know this is hard, but you have to see a doctor. It's part of filing charges."

I pulled away. "Let it go then. I don't want to file charges anyway, and it's my problem, not yours."

"This may have been your problem to begin with, but Mack is in the emergency room with a broken hand." Mom's voice had an edge to it, the same edge she'd had with me the night out on the deck when I was late. The same edge she got when she was trying to keep her cool but had had it with me. "Tasha thinks this is all her fault for not saying something sooner. I canceled two classes, and your father left a contract meeting. And in a little while I'm going to have to give Ali some sort of explanation as to why her big brother and sister look like they've been in a war zone. This is everyone's problem now. And you're done being in charge of how to solve it."

I stared out at the street, refusing to give in so easily. Even if she was right, I didn't like it, and I couldn't ignore that my new problem involved not only my family but Keith's family as well. And I didn't have a clue how to handle it any better than I was handling this. Mom stood back up. "Let's go."

Keith pulled up alongside the curb. He was too far away to see my bruises, but it wouldn't take long for him to figure out that something weird was going on. And after only a minute he cut the engine and got out of the truck. I looked at Mom.

She sighed. "You're not going to ride off with him, Miranda."

I knew that, but I couldn't help wishing it was that simple.

nineteen

"What happened?" Keith asked, the dimples disappearing when he got closer to Mom and me.

I was still sitting on the steps of the school, and I put my head down on my knees and started crying again. I was embarrassed about the way I looked, and I just couldn't face him. I heard Mom's voice, low and calm, explaining about Mike and the fight afterward. When she was finished I felt Keith's hand on my head. "Miranda, look at me."

I lifted my head, wiping my face the best I could, feeling the throb of my cheek when I touched it. "I'm sorry," I told him.

"Why? It's not your fault, okay?" His voice turned hard, a quality I'd never heard before. "I'm going to kill that jerk."

Mom heard it, too. "No, you're not, Keith." Her voice was sharp. "This is out of your hands. Miranda needs your support in other ways right now."

Keith took a deep breath, and for a second I thought he was going to argue with her, but he didn't. He put his arm around me but looked at Mom. "I'm sorry. You're right."

He held me against his shoulder, and I closed my eyes. I didn't want him to hurt like I was hurting. The nausea rose again and I pulled my head away from him to inhale the crisp, cool air.

"You're sick again, aren't you?" Mom asked me.

I shrugged. "Could I please just go home?"

"Keith," she said, "I need to get Miranda to a doctor, but she doesn't want to go. You think you can help me convince her?"

Keith stood up and held out his hand. "Come on, you need to go. I'll take you if your Mom will let me."

Mom hesitated. She'd already told me that I wasn't going to ride off with Keith, but she nodded. "Follow me."

At first we were silent in the truck. Keith drove with both hands on the wheel, and I leaned against the passenger door with my cheek on the window. The cool glass felt good against my swollen skin. I watched Mom's car in front of us and wondered when a good time would be to bring up the pregnancy test. Probably never.

The traffic light turned yellow. Mom went through the intersection, but Keith stopped. He looked over at me. "Did you think I'd be mad at you? Is that why you didn't say anything?"

I stared at him for a second, wondering how he'd guessed, but then adjusted back to the fact that he was talking about Mike. "I was embarrassed. I thought I brought some of it on myself because of Ryan, you know? And so I thought I had to handle it myself. What would you have done anyway?"

"I don't know, probably the same thing Mack did." Keith looked back at the light; it was still red and he met my eyes. "I hate that you were worried about something and didn't tell me. I want to be there for you."

The light changed and Keith turned his attention back to the road. I hoped that he really meant that.

He looked over at me. "Come here and let me hold you."

I wanted to slide over on the seat and let him put his arm over my shoulder. More than anything I wanted that, but I shook my head. He wouldn't want to hold me once he knew. I swallowed, trying not to burst into tears again, but the sobs were uncontrollable. Keith slowed the truck and pulled over to the curb. The hospital was just ahead; we were close enough to walk. I fumbled with the door handle, but Keith reached over and pulled me toward him. "Shh. Miranda, you're safe now. It's okay."

Maybe there in the truck in his arms I should've told him, but I glanced up and saw Mom waiting across the street for us. "I really don't think I can do this, Keith."

He thought I meant the doctor. "You've got to do this, Miranda.

I'll go with you and hold your hand. You'll be fine." He opened the door and held out his hand to me. I took it, promising myself that I'd tell him as soon as we were alone.

It always seems like I have to wait forever to see any doctor, and this time was no exception. Out of the corner of my eye, I could see the people in the waiting room checking out my battered face and swollen eyes. But I was thinking about what was happening inside my body, the stuff no one could see. When the nurse finally called my name, both Mom and Keith stood up with me. As much as I hated to, I let go of Keith's hand. "I'll do this alone," I told both of them.

They both looked uncertain, but the nurse said, "We'll get you if we need you."

Dr. Miller was our family doctor. She was a pro at handling sore throats, vaccinations, and delivering babies. Probably her most outstanding quality, though, was her ability to remain calm.

"What happened?" She said when she came into the room.

I explained about the fight, and she didn't flinch or exclaim. Instead she touched my cheek and examined the smaller purple marks on my arms from Mike's grip. Her fingers were warm, and it occurred to me that maybe she could help me with my bigger problem. Maybe she'd tell me that the grocery store tests weren't always reliable.

She made some notes on her clipboard and then met my eyes. "I don't think your cheekbone is fractured, but we should X-ray it to be on the safe side. And with the nausea we need to check for a concussion."

I hesitated for just a second. "I don't think I have a concussion. I've been queasy all day." She was listening attentively, but I still wasn't sure whether to trust her or not, but in a rush said, "You know those pregnancy tests at the grocery store? Are they accurate?"

She put her pen down and studied me. "Did you take one of

those tests? Is that what this fight was about?"

I shook my head. "The fight had nothing to do with it. The boy who hit me goes to my school. My boyfriend goes to Mountain View. He's in the waiting room with my mom. You can ask her. He didn't do this."

She gave a small nod and then sighed. "The tests are generally accurate, although there is a margin of error." Her gaze was intense, and I looked away, not wanting to cry in front of her.

"I started my period a week ago, but it only lasted a few hours. I took one of those tests today, and it was positive. How can I have a period and still be pregnant?"

Dr. Miller put the clipboard on the counter behind her and leaned forward with her hands on her lap. "Sometimes that happens. Do you remember when your last real period was?" Her voice was as matter-of-fact as if we were discussing the weather instead of my life. Somehow that calmed me, and I told her the date without panic rising in my voice. She took out a little round paper dial thing from a drawer and twirled it around a bit, then looked up at me. "It's been almost six weeks; we can see what's going on with an ultrasound. And I can give you an exam and take some blood to make sure everything is okay."

I waved toward the door. "What about my mom? Won't she know?"

The doctor shook her head. "What we discuss is confidential."

I shifted on the examining table, the paper rustling underneath me. I couldn't quite believe that I was having this conversation. My voice sounded like it belonged to someone else. "Could you do those tests, then? I mean just to make sure?"

She nodded. "I'm going to have to move you to another room. I'll tell your mom I'm going to observe you for a while. I was going to do that anyway. This is one of the worst bruises I've seen. I don't like releasing you without taking some X-rays to make sure your cheekbone is in one piece, but let's see where you are with this pregnancy, and then I'll make some decisions on your injury."

When she was pregnant with Ali, Mom had taken Mack and me to see her sonogram. I remembered the machine and the black and white fuzz on the small screen. Dr. Miller handed me a sheet and told me to slip out of my jeans. I stared up at the ceiling at a poster of fluffy, white kittens tumbling out of a basket while the doctor pressed on my abdomen and felt around inside me. She told me what she was checking for, but I didn't respond. When she was ready to do the sonogram, I closed my eyes. I remembered watching Ali float around; this time I didn't want to see anything at all.

"Yup," Dr. Miller said. "The test was right. Here's the heartbeat."

I looked at the screen where she was touching a blinking white dot with the end of her pen. I closed my eyes again, not comprehending that was really inside me.

"You can sit up," Dr. Miller told me after only a few minutes. She waited until I was looking at her before she said, "This has been a big day for you. I'm not at all comfortable sending you home. Your face is swollen now, and by morning I doubt you'll be able to see out of that eye. There's not much I can give you for the pain that's safe for early pregnancy." She paused a moment, but didn't break her gaze. "Let's tell your Mom, Miranda. I've known her a long time, and she can handle this. She'd want to know. I'll even tell her for you, if you want me to."

I blinked, trying not to bawl again. "What if I have an abortion though? Maybe my mom doesn't need to know." And it occurred to me that in the back of my mind somewhere I was already considering how to get out of this situation.

The doctor hesitated, but then said, "That is not a decision you can make right now, especially after the emotional trauma of a beating. What about your boyfriend? Does he know that you might be pregnant?"

I shook my head. "I didn't want to say anything until I knew for sure. And then when this happened," I touched my cheek, "I didn't have time."

"You have time now."

"I know. I'll tell him, I'm just not ready yet. Please don't make me." I put my hands up to my face to cover my sobs.

I felt Dr. Miller's hand on my shoulder. "Okay, Miranda. I'm going to talk to your Mom about caring for your injuries. Get dressed. Get a drink of water. I'll let you decide when to share your pregnancy."

I took my hands away from my face to thank her, but she wasn't finished. "If you're getting sick already, it might get worse before it's over. Your mom's had three kids, remember? It's not going to take her long to figure this out." She let this sink in before she continued, "This bruise is bad, but it'll heal. I believe that your boyfriend didn't hit you, but the situation at school is out of hand. The pregnancy is going to make your life even more complicated. You need help and emotional support no matter what decision you make. Tell your family."

Deep down I knew she was right, but when I headed out to the waiting room to face my family something happened to me. When I walked into the reception area, I had a flash of what my news would do to everybody. I saw the confusion in Dad's eyes and the pain in Mom's. I could feel Mack's shame and humiliation, Tasha's impatience and disgust, and Ali's astonishment.

I looked for Keith. He was fiddling with the zipper on his jacket, but when he noticed me he stood up and held out his hand, smiling with the dimples I loved so much. And just like that I knew that smile was going to disappear. I think I might have closed my eyes for a second, but in that blink I pushed all those images away. I told myself that I didn't have to hurt anyone. My blue-eyed knight and the rest of the cavalry didn't have to know. I'd deal with it on my own.

twenty

Because I'd thrown up at school, I expected to have a full-blown case of morning sickness. Aside from the fact that my eye was swollen shut, my cheek throbbed and my head was tender from contact with metal, I was fine when I woke up Friday morning. In fact I might not even have believed I could be pregnant, except for the pink line on the plastic test tube and the little white blip on the black screen that had permeated my dreams all night. I lay in bed listening for signs of who was awake, but all I noticed were the sounds of my own heartbeat and it made me think that somewhere inside of me another life was forming. I could pretend to everyone else that nothing was wrong, but there was no escaping my own mind.

Feeling sorry for myself seemed like a good way to spend the day, but Mom wouldn't let me stay in my room. She made me come down for lunch. Mack and I hadn't really talked since the fight because he'd been given a painkiller that made him sleepy. I was afraid he would hate me because he'd been suspended from school for three days, and his hand was broken in three places. But when I came into the kitchen he just let out at low whistle and said, "Wow. Good thing prom is six months away."

Dad shot him a look, but I laughed. "You're not going to win any beauty prizes either, buddy." In addition to the broken hand, he had a black eye and cut lip. "Will you be okay for baseball?"

He nodded. "I'll be fine. Are you okay?"

I nodded. I wanted to apologize to him. To them all, but I didn't even know where to begin. Ali was at school, so conversation didn't have to be guarded, but no one said much after that except for Dad asking me if I wanted more salad.

The sound of the doorbell broke the uncomfortable silence. It was a flower delivery—pink and red carnations and half a dozen white roses. They were from Keith and made me feel even worse about my secret. I touched the soft petals and knew I didn't deserve anything so beautiful. Not able to hold the vase and control my sobs at the same time, I shoved the vase toward Mom and fled to my room.

Expecting her to follow me, I wasn't surprised to hear the knock a few minutes later, but it wasn't Mom.

"Oh my God," Carly said, staring at my face. "Tasha said it was bad, but I had no idea."

"It looks worse than it feels," I said, drying my eyes and sitting up on my bed. I knew she wasn't there just to check on my injuries. She'd called every day to see if I'd changed my mind about taking the test. "Where's Josiah?"

"Downstairs watching cartoons with your brother. I saw your parents. They were loading the dishwasher. Your mom's been crying."

No wonder she didn't follow me. "This really messed them up."

"Well, I can see why they're upset. Tasha told me about how Mike's been treating you. What a jerk." She hesitated and then said, "Did you change your mind about taking the test?"

I met Carly's eyes but didn't have to say anything else. The tears that I swiped from my bruised cheek said enough.

Carly sighed. "Oh man. I was so hoping it would be a false alarm. I take it you haven't said anything to your parents yet?"

I shook my head. "And I'm not going to either. I can have an abortion whenever I can schedule it. It's safe after six weeks."

"Is that what Keith wants?"

"I don't know. It's what I want."

Carly stared at me. "You haven't told him?"

"Why ruin things? He doesn't need to know."

"Oh my God, Miranda, you have to tell him. This is his responsibility, too."

I didn't really know how to explain, but I tried. "Look. It was my mistake. I told him I thought it was a safe time. He trusted me. I'm not going to let him down."

"That's insane," Carly said, shaking her head. "He took a risk, same as you. He has a right to know. And what's going to happen when he finds out you lied to him?"

"He's not going to know, ever," I told her with a lot more conviction than I felt. "Look, Carly, I've heard stories about lots of girls keeping their pregnancies secret until delivering. It's on television all the time. I just need to keep mine secret for a few days. The clinic's only three blocks from here. I won't even need a ride. Nothing has to change."

"That's the craziest plan I've ever heard. And what if that's not what Keith wants? What if he wants you to have the baby?"

That was the first time the word baby had come up. I was doing my best to avoid thinking about babies. It was much easier to think of it not as a baby, but just as a problem that I needed to resolve. "Keith won't want a baby." But even as I said it, I wasn't sure. I'd seen him with the barn kittens and the ranch puppies that were always around. He'd cradle them and even kiss their heads. But kittens and puppies were a lot different from a baby. "Why would he want anything but an abortion? He's got his whole life ahead of him. Besides it doesn't really matter what he wants. It's my body."

Carly stood up and walked over to the window and looked out at the gray day, then turned back to me. "Danny wanted me to have an abortion. He begged, even."

She never talked about what happened with Danny, Josiah's father. I'd always been too afraid to ask, but now I said, "Why didn't you?"

She walked over to my dresser and took out one of the pictures I had tucked in the frame. I couldn't tell which one it was. "I thought if he loved me, he'd love our baby, too. I never thought he'd leave like he did." Carly put the picture back, but I thought I saw her wipe at her eyes. "And I just couldn't go through with an abortion."

"Why? Do you think it's wrong?" My voice was low and I wasn't sure I wanted to hear her answer.

She shook her head. "I think it's the right choice for some people. You know my friend, Tami? The one who went to the concert with us? She had an abortion."

"She did? When? Did you go with her?"

"It was about a year ago. Her boyfriend went with her. She doesn't talk about it much, but she'd probably answer your questions, if you had some." Carly came and sat on the bed next to me. "Having an abortion might be the right choice for you, Miranda. You're right. It is your decision, but I don't think you should make it without Keith. I know you're afraid of losing him, but you already have if you decide to lie to him."

I knew she was right, but I wasn't ready to admit it yet.

"Are you going to tell Tasha?"

This is the first secret I'd kept from Tasha. I was glad to have Carly, but I missed my best friend. "Do you think she'd tell Mack?"

"She's been your best friend longer than she's been Mack's girlfriend. She's worried about you and mad at herself for not stepping in when Mike first started hassling you."

I couldn't help smile. It was so like Tasha to think she could've handled the problem herself. But wasn't that what I always did, too? I took a deep breath and the nausea hit me just like it had in school—sudden and overpowering. I just made it to my bathroom. When I was finished, I rinsed out my mouth with cool water.

"Are you okay?" Carly asked from the doorway.

I nodded, but I felt shaky and staggered back to my bed. "I feel like I'm going to die." What if Mom had been with me instead? Dr. Miller was right. It wouldn't take Mom long to figure out where the nausea was coming from. "I don't think I'm going to be able to take much more of this, Carly."

She sat back on the bed, but before she could answer, Mom knocked on the door. I felt my insides freeze and I swiped at my eyes with the sleeve of my jersey, but I couldn't hide that I'd been crying.

Josiah ran to Carly and Mom said, "I'm sorry to interrupt, girls, but he was asking for you, Carly."

Carly scooped him up and cradled him against her shoulder. "It's okay. It's time for his morning nap, and we're going in a minute or two anyway."

Mom hesitated, her hand on the doorknob. "Are you all right, Miranda?"

I nodded and traded glances with Carly. Mom bit her lip, unconvinced. "Okay, I'll be in my room if you need anything…"

Carly let out a sigh when Mom left and settled on the floor with Josiah in her lap. She smoothed his hair, and he popped a thumb into his mouth. "I don't want to tell you what to do, but your mom is going to figure this out. And you're going to have to tell her anyway, Miranda. Since you're only sixteen, you might need a parent's consent. I know you're scared, but telling her won't be so bad. I know she'll help you, no matter what you decide." She hesitated for a minute, then said, "Your parents really helped me out when I had Josiah. They gave me money and your mom took me to the doctor once when my mom couldn't get off work."

"I don't think I have to tell her, Carly. I was doing some research on the Internet, and that parent consent law isn't enforced because of some court case. I just can't tell her about this. She asked me about birth control and I lied to her. She'd just die if she knew the truth. It's my fault, and I'll deal with it."

"It's not all your fault. Quit being so hard on yourself."

"I didn't mean for this to happen."

"I know you didn't." She looked down at Josiah. He was asleep. She kissed his temple, and I took that minute to brush a tear off my eyelash. "I wish there was something I could say to help you, Miranda."

I wished there was, too.

As if the day hadn't been bad enough, I still had to brace myself for Keith. I knew he'd be by after school, and for once in my life I was wishing Mom would step in and say, "No company." She'd done that with Ryan before and I'd been seething, but when the phone rang, she opened my door and said, "Miranda, it's Keith."

Because she was watching, I picked up my extension and said, "Hello." She didn't leave the room like I thought she would. Instead, she picked up the clothes I'd left on the floor and carried them to the hamper in my bathroom. She hadn't picked up after me since I was Ali's age.

"Feeling better?" Keith asked, unaware of my reluctance.

"I'm okay. Thanks for the flowers. They're beautiful." Mom came back and sat on the edge of my bed. Why couldn't she just leave me alone?

"Good. I'm glad you like them." He paused for a minute before asking, "Do you think you'd be up for dinner at my house tonight?"

I glanced at Mom, she was examining her chewed nails. "I don't know, Keith. I'm not sure I want your parents to see me like this. I don't even want you to see me like this."

Keith's voice was gentle. "I told them that you were hurt. Mom gave me the money for the flowers."

I closed my eyes and held my hand to my cheek. It was throbbing almost as much as when Mike first punched me. "You can't come over?"

"Probably not," Keith sighed. "My dad went to Greeley to look at a stallion that he might want to buy. He asked me to come home after to school and take care of the chores. I really want to see you, though, and make sure you're okay. You've been crying, haven't you?"

I took a deep breath. "A little. But I'm okay. We can see each other tomorrow, right?" To tell the truth, I was relieved. It was less of a lie when we weren't face to face.

"Yeah. I can come over in the morning."

"Maybe my parents would let me go over to your house." I glanced at Mom. I needed to get away from my room for a while, even though I wasn't sure hanging out at Keith's would be much easier.

Afterward, Mom asked, "He can't come over?"

"He has to help his dad. Would it be all right if I go over to his house tomorrow?"

She hesitated. "Well, we'll see how you're feeling. And you have to promise not to go anywhere else. No movies or hanging out downtown."

Like I really wanted to be seen in public—I couldn't see why I had to promise that. "Why?"

"Ryan will probably be home for Thanksgiving. We don't want you running into him."

I wasn't expecting that at all, but from the look on Mom's face, I could see that'd she'd been thinking about Ryan a lot.

"I can handle him," I said but I was sorry as soon as the words were out of my mouth. Even if I thought I could take care of it myself, that was the wrong thing to say.

"Miranda!"

"Well, what do you want me to do?" I couldn't keep the sarcasm out of my voice. Ryan was the least of my worries.

"We just want you to be careful. He might hear about what happened and try to talk to you."

My tough girl show crumpled. I dried off my tears with the edge of my sheet, but I couldn't get them to stop. Too late for careful now.

"I'm sorry, baby. I didn't mean to upset you." She wrapped her arms around me and rocked me like she used to when I was a little girl. I'd have given anything to go back to that time when her words always had the magic to solve all my problems.

twenty-one

Even though the crying jag drained me, I didn't get much sleep. I knew I'd have to argue with Mom if I wanted to leave the house, so as soon as the morning light hit the mountains, I slipped out of the house. The coffee machine didn't even have time to start and make me gag with the aroma.

Driving to Keith's ranch was like entering winter wonderland. The mountains were magical with white frost and falling crystals, and the house looked warm and cozy with a trail of smoke rising from the chimney. Keith opened the front door before I knocked, "Hi. You're early." I stepped into the warm living room and right into his hug, wondering the whole time if getting back into the cold Jeep would be the better choice.

Jody was sitting cross-legged in front of the fireplace, playing guitar. I hadn't seen her since that coffeehouse night. She looked better, not quite as wan. She was dressed in brown leather pants with a silky looking tank top. I couldn't tell if she was just coming in from a night out or heading out like that.

"Wow," she said, putting down the instrument and coming to hug me. "That looks bad."

Expecting that kind of reaction from Keith's family, I'd tried to look as nice as possible. Except for trimming the ends, I hadn't cut my hair since the concert, and it hung like honey down my back. A soft green sweater highlighted my eyes, and I chose my best-fitting jeans, but I could tell by Jody's shock that I hadn't really made an improvement. No amount of makeup would help with the bruise.

"Keith told me that your parents were pressing charges. That's so good, Miranda. He can't do this again, or next time it might be even worse."

I nodded, knowing that she was probably thinking about her rape. Dad had reassured me that Mike's behavior was not going unnoticed and that I'd be safe when I went back to school, but it was too much for me to think about. "Where are your parents?" I asked, hoping to change the subject.

I didn't miss the glance that Keith gave his sister before he told me, "They went skiing early this morning. Dad likes to go at least once before the holiday crowds start."

Jody raised her eyebrows. "You were supposed to tell her that last night."

Keith slid me a glance. "I tried, but she was sleeping. I didn't know she was going to come over so early, or I'd have left a message for her to call me before she left." He turned to me, blushing. "My parents didn't want us to be alone together for the entire day. Jody has to work."

Then I remembered Keith telling me she'd gotten a job at a music store, which explained the outfit. I was more surprised that Keith's parents were concerned about us being alone, but it made sense—our parents were a lot alike.

"I'm sorry. I should have called first."

Jody touched my arm. "It's okay, Miranda. It's not your fault, you didn't know."

Keith squeezed my hand. "We can go back to your house. I'll need to check on the horses though. I promised my dad."

Going back to my house was the last thing I wanted to do. I used all my charm on Jody. "Please, let us stay." I waved my hand toward the window. "My parents don't like me driving in the snow anyway, so I'll leave early, before it gets icy. I promise we'll behave ourselves."

Keith nodded, too. "We haven't had a chance to talk most of the week." He blushed, but didn't let go of my hand. "We'll be good."

Jody shrugged. "I don't care if you stay, Miranda." She gave

Keith a light punch on the shoulder. "Please be careful. I can't afford to have this on my conscience, too; I'm running out of room in that area of my brain."

I felt a twinge of my own conscience. I could relate to an overload in that department.

The kitchen at the ranch extended the whole length of the house, with its large windows overlooking the riding arena and pastures. Deer had jumped the fence and were in the pasture. The falling snow filtered down in tiny crystals, evaporating before reaching the ground. I sat at the round oak table across from Keith and watched him slice the still-warm homemade bread. The crust flaked onto the table. It was a winter fairy tale everywhere except in my mind. I almost wished that Keith and I had gone to my house. At least Ali would have been around for a distraction. I never realized how hard it was to say anything without saying everything.

"I forgot to tell you, Miranda, new puppies were born yesterday. They're out in the barn. Want to go see them?" Keith told me after taking a huge swallow of milk.

I didn't want to think about babies of any kind, but I knew gushing over the puppies was unavoidable. At least it was a distraction from serious conversation. "What are we waiting for?" I asked.

The new puppies were tiny and black, and nursing. Their mama, a large Labrador, looked up at us and thumped her tail twice against the horse blanket. Keith grinned at me. "Would you like one?"

I didn't even know how to answer that question, but I shrugged and said, "Maybe." The mama and baby scene was too much for me. Not to mention the overpowering aroma of hay, horses, and leather. It was all I could do to force back the gags. Hoping I wasn't being obvious I nodded toward the ATVs parked by the entrance to the barn and said, "We could take those out for a ride."

Keith shrugged. "Well, it'll be cold, but if you want."

I'd never had much interest in ATV riding before, and I was surprised at how much fun it was tearing through the pastures in the falling snow. Part of the appeal might have been that conversation was impossible. Concentrating on navigating around the rocks and through the snowflakes made me forget my problems for most of the morning.

When we came inside, Keith built the dying fire into a blazing roar and then went to make hot cinnamon apple cider. I sank back into cushions in front of the stone hearth and stared into the flames. So far I'd put on a good show, pretending nothing was wrong, but it was exhausting me. I closed my eyes wishing that I could just wish it all away. I didn't even hear Keith until I felt his arms go around me. "Are you sleeping?" he whispered.

I snuggled into his arms, but faced away from him. I knew his sweet, slow kisses would turn into something more. As much as I wanted to forget the bruises on my face, I didn't think anything would take away the nagging secret in my head. Keith kissed my shoulder and hugged me tight. "Thanks for coming over today. I've really missed you."

I rolled over on my side to face him. "Me too."

"You're really okay? I've been worried about you."

I nodded, afraid my voice might give away the truth.

He kissed my forehead, and I closed my eyes. I couldn't look at him, he was being so serious. He kissed my eyelids, then my mouth. I had to kiss back or risk letting him in know something was really wrong. When he put his hand on the top button of my jeans, I whispered, "I thought we were being good today."

"You're right." But he kissed my stomach underneath my belly button before stretching out next to me.

My stomach was flat, and I knew he couldn't tell anything, but I touched the spot where his lips had been, wondering if every one of his touches would trigger some reminder of my secret.

"Is something wrong, baby?" he asked me, putting his hand on top of mine.

I hesitated a split second before making my choice, I reached up and ran my fingers through his hair, kissing his throat. "Do you have condoms?" I whispered.

"In my room."

I let him lift me up and carry me down the hall. How could I let him believe for a moment that we had to worry about birth control? What was wrong with me?

Keith's hand was on my stomach when I jerked awake. I had just been dreaming that Ali was a baby again, sick with colic. Mom had thrust her into my arms and stood back watching me cope with the screams. I was begging for help when I realized the baby wasn't my sister. It was another child with honey hair like mine and blue eyes like Keith's.

"What's wrong, baby?" Keith asked me.

"Just a dream," I said, hoping he wouldn't ask for details. "I didn't mean to wake you up."

"You didn't. I was just watching you." He propped his head up on one hand and put his other one on my breast under the sheet. "You're amazing, you know that?"

"Mmmm," I said, making it sound like a purr instead of a wince. My breasts were too sore for much touching, so interlocking his fingers with mine, I brought his hand to my mouth and kissed his fingers. "You're pretty amazing yourself."

The shades in the room were drawn, but my eyes were adjusted to the dimness, and I knew Keith well enough to know that he was blushing. "You're just saying that to make me feel better."

"No, Keith, you're great." I meant that, too. He might be the inexperienced one, but I was the one learning what it was like to be with someone I loved. It seemed amazing to me that I could've ever shared my body with someone I hadn't loved.

In a voice I barely recognized as my own, I whispered, "Keith, I need to tell you something."

He caught the change in my expression right away and loosened his hold. "What's wrong, baby?"

There was no easy way to start. I gathered up a pillow and sat hugging it to my chest, but I couldn't meet his eyes. Instead, I looked at the jumble of our jeans and socks on the floor by the bed. "You know a couple of weeks ago when I told you my period started?"

"Yeah?" His voice was cautious, like he was afraid of where this was going.

"Well, it only lasted a couple of hours. When I woke up later that night, it was over." I glanced at him again. He was playing with the edge of the sheet, but he looked up at me when I paused. I was going to continue, but I didn't have to.

"What does that mean? That you're pregnant?"

I nodded, hugging the pillow harder, trying to tough it out and not cry. I never wanted him to hold me more than at that moment, but he got up and untangled his jeans from mine. I didn't want him to walk away from me, but I was finally waking up to the fact that I wasn't in control of his side of the story. Keith picked up a baseball from on top of his dresser and slapped it into the palm of his hand. He was turned away from me, and I couldn't read his expression.

"I'm sorry, Keith. This is all my fault."

"No, Miranda. It's not." He turned back to me and crossed the room. Sitting on the bed again, he put one hand around my ankle. "I knew this could happen. I just hoped it wouldn't."

"Yeah, but, that night I said—"

"You said you just finished your period, I know. I remember. But that probably wasn't exactly right, was it?"

I nodded. "Why didn't you say something then, if you knew?"

"I wanted to keep going just as much as you did." He blushed. "When you have your period, you carry that tiny leather backpack. You left it open once, and I saw the tampons. That night when we were driving home, I tried to figure out when you had the backpack last, and I realized it might not have been such a safe time."

"But you never said anything."

"Neither did you. I figured if you weren't worried, maybe I was wrong."

"I've been terrified, but I didn't want you to be mad. I thought about not telling you and just dealing with it myself," I said, not meeting his eyes.

"How could you even think that?" His voice got hard like it had on the steps at school. I knew he was angry. He let go of my ankle and moved away from me. "I would have never talked to you again if you had done that. This is just like that jerk Mike. Why do you keep secrets from me?"

He was right to be angry, but I didn't know what to say and the tears that seemed to be always at the surface these days let go. I just wanted out of there, but it's hard to flee without clothes and even harder to get dressed while sobbing. Keith didn't seem to realize that I was making a getaway until I'd managed to pull on my sweater and jeans. "Where are you going, Miranda? You can't run away from this."

But I could run away, and that's what I was going to do. I pushed past him and made a break for the living room where I thought I'd left my keys. My vision was blurring; I swiped at my face, forgetting about my cheek. The touch caused instant throbbing, but I didn't care. I deserved the pain.

Keith caught up to me, just when I found the keys underneath the cushions in front of the dying fire. All he had to do was grab my arm or block my path, and I wouldn't have been strong enough to escape, but he didn't. Instead he reached for my hand, his touch light and easy. "I'm sorry. I'm not mad, okay? Please don't go."

I didn't resist when he put his arms around me, but I kept crying with my fists against his chest. He held me tighter than he ever had, until I was all cried out and was holding him, too.

"Keith," I said into his chest, "I'm sorry. I really didn't mean for this to happen."

"I know, baby. We'll figure it out, okay? Are you positive you're pregnant?"

Moving out of his arms, I nodded. "The doctor who looked at my cheek gave me an exam. I'm about six weeks along."

He took a deep breath. "Okay. So what are we going to do?"

"How do you feel about abortion?" I asked, glancing at him to gauge his reaction.

He plopped on the couch. "I never thought I'd be the kind of guy to ask someone to do that." His voice was low, and he sounded close to crying.

Going over next to him, I put my hand on his thigh. "You're not asking me. It's what I want. Don't you think it would be the best choice?"

Keith didn't answer right away. Instead he put his hands behind his head and stared up at the ceiling for a minute or two. "I guess I just always thought that abortion was wrong." He looked at me to see how I was taking this and then said, "I can't just turn that off, especially when we were so reckless that night."

I stared at him. "You think we deserve this?"

"I don't know, but I think we have an obligation to see it through now."

"God, Keith. Please don't tell me that. There's no way I can do anything else."

He tried to take my hand, but I moved off the couch and went to the window. The snow was a lot heavier than in the morning. The mountains were barely visible and I wondered if the storm would keep me trapped on the ranch. A week ago that would have been a dream come true.

Keith joined me at the window. "I just can't help thinking we should at least consider the alternatives."

"What alternatives, Keith?" I stared at him, not quite comprehending how he could even say that. "You're not the one who has to gain a million pounds and be sick and walk through the halls of school being laughed at and whispered about."

"I know that," he said, "but—"

"But what? Do you want to tell your parents about this? The reason they don't want us to be alone for any length of time is they're afraid something like this is going to happen. Mine feel the same way. This would kill them."

"Our parents would be rocked, but they'd survive. They'd help us, you know they would."

"Oh yeah, I can see my mom knitting baby blankets. She'll be thrilled." I tried a new approach. "Don't you want to go to college next year, Keith?"

He shrugged, "You know college isn't that important to me. I could get a job for a year or two first. We could make this work, Miranda."

And I thought I was the one living in a dream world. I turned away from him, staring out into the cold whiteness.

After what seemed like hours, he said, "I guess I understand why you didn't want to tell me. You've already made up your mind that I don't get to be a part of this decision."

The truth of his words stung. I closed my eyes and gathered my courage to face him. He was standing with his arms crossed, kicking the carpet with his bare foot. A single tear ran down his cheek.

"I'm sorry, Keith." Hoping that he wouldn't pull away, I put my hand on his arm. "I guess I'm just really scared."

"Me too." He covered my hand with his. "And maybe what you want is the right thing, but I need some time."

"I promise I won't shut you out anymore. We'll decide together." Those two sentences were some of the hardest words I've ever had to say. And while driving home those words kept replaying in my head. The windshield wipers on the old Jeep could hardly keep up with the snow and the defroster wasn't working well enough to keep ice from blurring my vision. It took all my effort to stay on the road at a crawl. And just for a moment, I wondered if driving off the canyon road into the blizzard might just be the best solution all the way around.

twenty-two

"Miranda, the parade is on," Ali told me, pulling on my arm at six o'clock Thanksgiving morning.

"That's nice." I didn't even open my eyes, although keeping Ali out of everyone's hair during dinner preparations is my annual contribution to a day that's far more than a national holiday around my house. Dad begins his display of culinary genius at dawn and the guests sometimes come as early as kick-off for the first bowl game. The event had been toned down a little because of the fight at school—just Tasha's family and Keith's family—but I still had no desire to get up and pretend life was grand.

"Come on, aren't you going to watch it with me?"

"No." I thought Ali ought to wake Keith up a couple of mornings in a row, he'd change his mind about the whole kid thing pretty fast. The promise to consider each other's point of view hadn't really gotten us anywhere. I hadn't changed my mind, and Keith was still torn.

"You never do anything with me anymore," she accused me with her best whine.

Whining always works real well for Ali. Mack and I will do almost anything to make her stop. "Fine, I'll watch the stupid parade." I whipped off my comforter and sat up too fast. My stomach lurched, and I hurried into the bathroom with my hand over my mouth. I was just grateful that Ali wasn't old enough to get the connection.

"Are you okay?" Ali asked, stepping just inside the door. "I'll get Mom."

"No!"

At the risk of getting sick again, I reached for my sister and yanked her far enough inside so that I could shut the door. "Don't tell Mom anything." Ali's eyes started to water, and she was rubbing her arm where I'd grabbed her. I never hurt Ali before, and I was as stunned as she was. I sank back against the door and wiped sweat off my forehead. She backed away, out of my reach.

My words came out in a rush, desperate. "I'm sorry, Ali-cat. I didn't mean it. Honest. Please don't tell anyone I'm sick. Mom might cancel Thanksgiving if she found out. It's from getting hit on the head that day at school. The doctor said it might happen for a while, but it makes Mom and Dad and Mack worried. So let's let it be our secret."

Ali weighed my words and examined her arm. It wasn't marked at all. Finally she said, "Your bruise is getting better." The shower door was mirrored, and I looked at myself. The bruise didn't hurt anymore and most of it had settled into a greenish yellow color. The bright purple part had faded into an eggplant shade. I didn't think it would be all faded by the time I went back to school, but enough to be covered with makeup. Ali leaned back against the shower door, blocking my reflection. "Mom knows you're sick. She told Daddy that you need to go back to the doctor. Daddy said to wait a few more days."

Good old Dad. I could always count on him for denial. "Dad's right, Ali. I'll be fine in a few more days. Promise me you won't tell Mom?"

"Okay, but are you going to watch the parade with me?"

"Sure." Like I had a choice.

After the parade was over and football took over the television, it was all I could do to keep my eyes open. I never knew pregnancy would make me so sleepy, but I was afraid to give in to the nap that was calling to me. First of all, Ali might still blab to Mom, and I was terrified of sinking into yet another horrifying dream of babies and small children. So I let Ali lead me up to her room, deciding that she might distract me from playing out my options for the millionth time. I flopped on her bed while she dragged out Tiddly Winks, Checkers, and Old Maid. I looked around the room, really seeing it for the first time. Most of her stuff had been either Mack's or mine at some point. There was nothing really "Ali" in it, except for the jungle animal comforter Mom had bought her over the summer. I had a sudden inspiration.

"Let's make a jungle on the wall behind your bed, Ali."

She put the games on the bed and hopped up next to me. "What?"

"Yeah. We could turn it into a rainforest. Big trees and flowers, and monkeys. You'd fall asleep every night with them guarding you."

Getting into the spirit of the idea, Ali said, "What about jaguars and parrots with blue and yellow feathers? And an elephant?"

"I don't think elephants live in the rainforest, but sure." I got off the bed to see where to begin. The wall was just plain white with a lone barnyard animal print. I took it down and leaned it next to the wastepaper basket.

"Do you think Mom will care?" Ali asked.

I shook my head. "Nope. I painted my room, and she didn't get mad." Mom would probably be thrilled that I was doing something besides sleeping. I was thrilled to have something other than myself occupying my thoughts for a change.

To keep Ali busy, I made a stencil of an elephant and a parrot and had her trace them on the wall above her bed while I covered all the furniture and floor with old sheets. I outlined the rest of the scene and found some paint in the garage to get us started. The paint fumes didn't make me sick and for the first time in a long time, the hours slipped away.

"Miranda?" Ali asked, breaking into my concentration.

"Yeah?"

"How do you make trees look like trees?"

I looked down at her, she was sitting on the floor watching me on the ladder.

Leaving my paint tray on the shelf, I climbed down and sat with her. "Most people just draw brown lines up and then put a green cloud on top, but that's not what trees really look like, right? Instead the branches twist out and up and the leaves are alike but different, and they cover each other and bits of light show through. You have to remember all those things when you do trees."

Ali nodded. "What grade did you learn that in?"

I shrugged. "I don't think I learned about drawing trees at school. It's just something I know how to do."

"Do you think I'll ever learn how?"

Studying the elephant, I noticed her brush strokes were even and clean for a seven-year-old, but then she'd been coloring with me forever. "Keep practicing, Ali, and you'll learn."

She looked at me to test my seriousness, then she said, "I'm scared you're going to get hurt again when you go back to school."

The catch in her voice surprised me, and I put my arms around her and held her tight. "I won't. A lot of people will be watching to make sure I'm okay."

"It was really scary to see your face all black and blue. I had a bad dream about it, and Mom slept with me."

I rested my chin on her head so she wouldn't see my eyes watering and said, "I'm sorry, Ali."

She sniffed. "Do you think that will happen to me when I get to high school?"

I closed my eyes, wanting to just disappear. "Listen, Ali-cat," I said after a moment or two, shifting so I could look into her serious brown eyes. "You'll be okay. I'll be watching out for you."

"Promise?"

I nodded.

"Do you think you could show me how to make wrinkles in the elephant's skin?"

It was easy enough to take my brush and make small lines and shadows in the elephant's trunk and legs and ears. I wondered how I'd ever be able to show my little sister that she didn't have to make the same mistakes I'd made.

Tasha came up sometime later with some fruit and crackers. She winked at Ali. "Want to go play with Josiah for awhile?"

"I'm a little busy here," Ali told her in a very sassy voice.

Tasha raised her eyebrows. "I'll give you two bucks."

Ali looked at me.

"It's okay. You did a great job on the elephant." When she left, I turned to Tasha. "What was that all about?"

She shrugged. "Carly said you wanted to talk to me. I figured we might not get another chance later."

I nodded and got back up on the ladder with my tray of green paint. I decided it would be easier to tell Tasha if I wasn't looking at her.

Instead she surprised me. "Did Mack tell you about our science project?"

I shook my head, even though he might have told me. Conversations weren't staying in my head very well.

"We're building our own rainforest ecosystem. I got on the Internet on your Dad's computer this morning to look up a couple of plants we want to use, and I saw abortion sites in the history log."

"Did Mack see them?" I asked, scared for the answer.

She shook her head. "I deleted them from the log."

I sat down on one of the bottom rungs of the ladder, sighing. "You must think I'm really dumb, huh?"

"Only when you say stuff like that. How long have you known?"

"For a while. Keith wants me to have the baby."

"And you don't." That's the great thing about Tasha. No long explanations are ever necessary; she can really see the whole picture. "Why not?"

I shrugged. "A lot of reasons. I don't want to go to school pregnant. I don't want to disappoint Mom and Dad again. Obviously if I'm not mature enough to make good decisions about sex, how can I make decisions about a child?"

Tasha picked up the gray paint Ali'd been using and wiped the brush on the edge of the tray. "Come on, Miranda, that's not like you—well-rehearsed reasons. I would have guessed that an abortion would be the last thing you would've wanted. I mean all that happily ever after stuff. You like kids. I know you act like taking care of Ali is the biggest inconvenience of your life, but you're always good to her. Who else would think of something like painting a rainforest?"

I shrugged, but Tasha was right. I'd never been good at logical reasoning, but I'd had some practice in coming up with arguments for why abortion was the best choice. They sounded more plausible than the truth: I was terrified at how out of control my life had gotten. I just couldn't cope with more chaos. "I don't know if I can explain it, Tasha."

"Try."

I took a deep breath and got off the ladder and sat on the floor next to her. "I know I always talk about forever and stuff, but that's like white horses and sunsets, nothing as real as this. This is most real thing that's ever happened to me. I always think I can handle everything, but for once I realize there's no way I'm ready for this."

We were silent for a moment and then I said, "I know what you're thinking, Tasha. I should've thought this all through before I hopped into bed. I know I really screwed up this time."

"I don't think that at all, Miranda. I mean two months ago, I would've agreed with that statement. But since I've been with Mack, I guess I understand more."

"Are you guys—?" I asked, studying her expression carefully.

"No, not even close, but I can see how it happens." She caught my eye. "I just don't want you to make a mistake you're going to regret for the rest of your life. An abortion is final; there's no going back."

"I know. I've been lying awake at night going over all the options in my head. And I always come back to the same answer. Keith thinks because we weren't careful we have an obligation to accept the responsibility. Do you think he's right?"

"I don't know. I understand what he means, but I don't believe having a baby should be seen as an obligation. That makes it sound like a punishment or something."

"When I first found out, I just wanted it to be over. I didn't want to think about how it felt to have something growing inside of me, but I can't stop now. It's like something completely out of my control has taken over my body. Maybe it would be beautiful and amazing if I wanted it, but now it just terrifies me." I dashed at my eyes.

"Have you told Keith that?"

"I think so, but I don't know. It's easier to talk about it with you. I always end up getting so emotional with him. I probably make no sense."

Tasha sort of smiled. "I doubt that." She then added, "Maybe this isn't something that can be compromised."

I took a deep breath. "I know. I'm afraid our relationship isn't going to survive this."

She sighed. "I wish I could help more."

"I know."

We were still sitting there, not painting, when Mom came up to tell us to get ready for dinner. "Something wrong?" she asked, taking in how serious we were.

I shook my head. It was getting harder and harder for me to speak around Mom. Everything I said seemed like a lie.

Tasha said, "We're just hungry."

Mom nodded and took in the transformation on the wall. "Wow, that looks great, Miranda."

"So it's okay then?"

She raised her eyebrows. "Well, if you were really concerned about that, you'd have asked first, right?" But she winked at me, and I could tell she thought I was back to my old self. I was only too happy to let her.

Keith and I sat next to each other through dinner but didn't get a chance to be alone until late in the evening. We settled on the staircase in the living room high enough away to have privacy but close enough to show that we weren't making out.

"How are you feeling?" Keith asked. We were holding hands and sitting close, so we could keep our voices low even though no one was within earshot.

"Wiped out. How about you?"

"About the same." He squeezed my hand. "I told my sister. She totally agrees with you. She told me that I'd completely lost my mind. Sometimes I think I have."

Putting my head against Keith's shoulder for a minute I said, "I don't think you've lost your mind. I dream about the baby." I didn't tell him the dreams were more like nightmares. "Tasha knows, too. She didn't really give me an opinion either way."

Keith nodded toward the living room. "It'd be really hard to go down there and tell the rest of them, wouldn't it? They'd all have a different opinion about what we should do."

We watched the scene for a while in silence. Our dads were playing chess and our moms were sitting on the couch with Tasha's mom. Jody was playing guitar for Ali and Josiah and teaching them some folk songs. Mack and Tasha were trying to help by singing along. They were all laughing a lot. Carly was missing the fun because she had to go to work. The restaurant where she waited tables didn't close on the holidays.

"How much is an abortion anyway?" Keith whispered.

I shrugged. "I don't know. Four hundred dollars is what I saw on the Internet."

He let out a low whistle. "That's some fucking Christmas present."

I stared at him. I'd never heard him swear like that before.

He squeezed my hand. "I'm sorry. I'm just still having a really hard time with the whole idea. I can't get away from feeling like I'm running away from my responsibility."

I looked back down the stairs at our families, thinking about my conversation with Tasha. Even though I knew I should try and explain how overwhelmed I felt, I found myself bringing up the small things again. "No matter how many times I try to imagine it another way, I can't get past facing the hallways at school and seeing my parents disappointed. I just don't want to be pregnant a minute longer than I have to."

He sighed. "Maybe we could talk to someone. Like an abortion counselor or something. I have some questions."

I could feel my insides lighten, maybe he was coming around. "Okay. I'll call and see if we can get an appointment tomorrow or next week."

Late that night, after everyone was gone, I went in to look at the progress I'd made in Ali's room. It'd been so easy for me to whip up the fantasy of a rainforest world. Touching the wet paint, I realized that a gallon of white paint could erase in a matter of minutes the work I'd done. Ali was asleep in my spare bed, so I slipped into my jersey without turning on the light. Under the covers, I pressed my fingers into my flat stomach. An abortion would wipe out the life Keith and I created in a matter of minutes. Even if that's what I wanted, I'd never be able to forget the power of what was going on inside me. I fell asleep with tears still sliding down my cheeks.

twenty-three

The waiting room at the abortion clinic wasn't much different from Dr. Miller's office, except the receptionist was behind bullet-proof glass and there was a buzzer system on the doors. Keith picked up a magazine, but I rested my head on his shoulder, sleepiness overwhelming me once again. I heard the counselor call my name, and I rubbed my eyes and stifled a yawn before standing up. She said her name was Elizabeth and ushered us back to a room with a couch and a couple of chairs. After gathering some basic facts, she set her clipboard on the small table next to her chair and turned her full attention to us.

"I gather you aren't here to chat. So how can I help you?"

Keith took a deep breath and asked about the procedure. Elizabeth launched into a play-by-play, using and explaining technical terms like evacuation and dilation. She showed us some tools on a stainless steel tray. It reminded me of the tray of tools at the dentist's office, only larger. I felt sort of sick to my stomach, and I really didn't take in the rest of her words.

Elizabeth stopped in mid-sentence. "Are you all right, Miranda?"

"I just need some water. I'll get some from that drinking fountain in the hall." I lingered in the hall for a minute more than I needed to catch my breath. I didn't need to hear about the process. I just needed it to work.

Keith took my hand when I joined him back on the couch. "You okay, babe?"

"Yeah. What are we talking about now?" I asked, feigning interest.

"Keith asked about complications," Elizabeth answered. "I told him they are rare in the early stages, but the risk goes up as the pregnancy progresses. Are you getting nauseated often, Miranda?"

Before answering, I glanced at Keith. We hadn't talked about my symptoms much. I hoped he wouldn't think I was keeping secrets from him again. "Some. There's no pattern to it."

Elizabeth tapped her fingers on the arm of her chair. The cushion absorbed the sound. Little details were making me lose focus of the conversation, but her next question caught my total attention. "Why not adoption?"

Keith and I looked at each other. That was the one thing we agreed on. If we agreed to have the baby, we were keeping the baby.

"It's not an option," I said, without wavering or explaining.

Elizabeth seemed on the brink of exploring that response, but Keith jumped back to the abortion questions. "Do I get to be with Miranda during the procedure?"

"Why is that important to you?" Elizabeth asked him. I tried to keep my focus on Keith's profile. It was strange to see him without his smile.

He seemed to struggle with his thoughts. "I just don't think I could sit on a couch in the waiting room reading the latest edition of *Sports Illustrated* while Miranda is...well, you know." He ran his fingers through his hair. "I just want to be there for her if she needs me..." Keith was trying hard to control the emotion in his voice.

Elizabeth made a note on her clipboard and then said, "The doctors here don't allow anyone in the procedure room but the patient and medical staff. There are clinics that allow the patient to make the choice if she'd like a support person with her. Is that important to you, too, Miranda?"

"Sure. I guess." Actually, I hadn't given it much thought. Looking at Keith, I wondered if I wanted him with me. I thought about Dr. Miller giving me the exam. I'd stared up at the ceiling when she'd put the instrument inside of me. Keith would see me on the table like that, which in many ways seemed even more intimate than holding his body close to mine.

Elizabeth put down her clipboard. "Keith, I'd like to talk to Miranda alone for a few minutes. Would you mind sitting in the room next door?"

He looked at me. I knew he didn't want to go and I didn't want him to either, but I squeezed his hand. "It's okay, babe."

The counselor stood up and held the door for Keith. When she sat back down, she took a hard look at me and said, "Is this really what you want, Miranda? I can't help but notice you're not the one asking questions."

I shook my head, amazed that she got the facts so wrong. "The abortion is my idea. Keith's asking all the questions because he isn't sure it's the right thing."

"That looks like the remains of a fist print on your face. How did it happen?"

My hand went automatically to the bruise. "It happened at school. A guy I know. It doesn't have anything to do with Keith. He'd never hurt me like that."

I couldn't tell if she believed me or not, but she let Keith come back in.

Keith and I were silent on the drive home. The clinic was only three blocks from my house, but Keith turned south on Broadway and drove past downtown and through campus before heading for my street. The afternoon traffic wasn't too heavy, but we seemed to hit all the red lights. The stop-and-go motion made me queasy, and I was drained from the counseling session. Even worse was the feeling that it hadn't helped the decision at all.

We were almost at my house when he finally spoke. "Did the counselor ask you if I gave you that bruise?"

I turned to him, but his eyes were on the road. "Yeah, she did."

"She asked me too, when you were getting a drink." Keith turned onto my street and parked against the curb. He turned to face me. "I don't want to go back there."

I closed my eyes and put my head back against the seat. "Keith, I can't take much more of this. Why can't you just let me do this?"

Sighing, he laced his fingers behind his head. "I told a guy I know about this. He told me I was insane and that I should just pay for the whole thing and count myself lucky that you want an abortion. But I just can't make myself feel that way. It's our baby, Miranda. Don't you see that?"

With my eyes brimming, I turned to him. "I see the baby every night in my dreams. She calls out to me, and I'm never close enough to comfort her. I saw her heartbeat on the sonogram screen. I'll never forget that. But still, Keith, I can't..." My voice broke, and I tried to open the door before the deluge of sobs hit.

The automatic door locks stalled my exit. Keith reached for me. "Miranda, wait, I'm not finished." Fumbling for the release button, I escaped and ran to the house. Mom was in the living room, but I rushed past her up to my room. I knew she'd follow me, but I didn't have any other place to go.

Mom didn't say anything for a long time. She just sat next to me on the bed, with her hand on my back, and let me cry. When she did speak, her voice was gentle. "What's going on, Miranda?"

"Nothing," I said into my pillow. "I'll be fine."

"Yeah, I can see that."

I just sobbed harder.

"You're going to make yourself sick."

She was right about that. My head was pounding, and I felt more nauseated than I had since Mike had punched me. "I can't tell you, Mom. Please, for once just leave me alone."

"No, Miranda, I'm not going to leave you alone."

I knew she wouldn't either, but I just couldn't face her.

"Is it Ryan?"

I shook my head, still clutching my pillow tight.

"Did you and Keith have a fight?"

"No!" I turned over and screamed. "I don't want to talk about it. Don't you get that?"

I've got to hand it to Mom. She stayed right there with me, totally in control, and without a trace of anger in her voice. "Don't shout at me. I get that you don't want to talk about it, but you're going to have to, or I'll make Keith tell me."

She was serious, and Keith would tell Mom if she pressed him. Knowing it would be better coming from me, I sat up and hugged my knees toward my chest, but I couldn't speak. Mom watched me trying to catch my breath, and then got up and went into my bathroom. I heard the water running in the sink. I closed my eyes. I'd stashed a box of crackers in the towel closet to fight the nausea. If she saw it, she might make the connection on her own. I wouldn't be forced to say the words.

If she saw the crackers, she made no mention of them. The warm washcloth she handed me was clean. Our eyes locked, and I looked away, eyes brimming again. Her voice was soft when said, "Miranda, please tell me. I can't stand to see you hurting like this."

That was too much for me, and I covered my face with my hands, choking on the words, "I just can't tell you, Mom. You'll hate me."

"No, I won't." Then in a quiet voice, she asked, "Are you pregnant? That's what this is about, isn't it? Nothing else could upset you this much."

Using the washcloth to hide my shame, I sobbed, "I'm so sorry, Mom."

"Oh, baby." She took me in her arms, smoothing my hair with her hands.

"Mom, you were so right about all this," I said, not even trying to hold back a new troop of sobs. "I'm so not ready for something this big. Why didn't I listen?"

"Don't say things like that, Miranda. It doesn't do any good." She didn't let go of me, but she sat back a little and moved my hair out of my eyes. "Did you just tell Keith?"

I shook my head. "No, we went to an abortion clinic to talk to a counselor. Keith thinks we should have the baby. But I just can't have a baby now. I just can't."

I saw shock spread across Mom's face. "How far along are you, Miranda?"

"Seven, going on eight weeks."

Mom closed her eyes and then got up and went to the window. "I knew you were covering something up, but I thought it had to do with that fight at school. I should have known. I was sleepy and sick like you've been every time I was pregnant."

Wringing the washcloth in my hands, I looked over at Mom. She was crying without making a sound. "I'm sorry, Mom. I never wanted to upset you. That's why I didn't want to tell you. I wasn't going to tell anyone, not even Keith."

"Miranda, how can you even say that? You can't go your whole life thinking you can handle everything yourself. That's so selfish. Your choices affect everyone around you. You can't keep ignoring that. What about Keith's feelings?"

"I'm trying, Mom. But I don't understand why he wants a baby when we've got our whole lives ahead of us."

She turned from the window to face me. "Now you have another life to consider."

"So you think I should have the baby, too?"

"I didn't say that, Miranda."

"So you think I'm right?"

"I didn't say that either. I just think you have to make an informed choice and not just alter your body because you're in a rush to go back to the way things were. That's not going to ever happen. You may not want what Keith wants, but you made a conscious choice to share your body with him. Now you have to share the decisions that come with that choice."

I didn't rush right in with a response, allowing her words to soak in. "What do you think I should do?"

She came and sat on my extra bed. "I'd like to tell you what to do, but this isn't something I can fix for you." She bit her lip and then said, "I do know what it's like to be unexpectedly pregnant."

I met her eyes, realizing she was going to share something private with me.

"Mack was only six weeks old when I found out that I was pregnant with you. And Ali was just a shock. Both times I remember walking around wondering how I was going to cope…"

I cut in, thinking she was finished. "Did you consider not having me? Or Ali?"

She didn't hesitate. "Not for a second. The timing wasn't great, but I was thrilled all the same. I had your dad and having kids was always in our plans. I never had to face the choice you're facing."

"Mom?" My voice sounded small and scared, even to me. "Do you think abortion is wrong?"

She didn't answer right away. "I think that's a question you have to answer for yourself. What can you live with?"

I wiped my face and took a moment or two to think about my words. "At first I thought abortion was an easy fix, but I know I was wrong about that. I know it isn't just going to make everything disappear. In fact, I know living with the decision might be just as hard as having a baby. I have these dreams at night, Mom—" My voice broke and Mom moved over onto my bed and put her arm around me, but I struggled to continue wanting her to understand. "It's like being in a nightmare all the time. I know I've made lots of bad choices, but this time I know this is right for me."

"And Keith?"

Before I could answer, there was knock on the door.

Mom left the bed, opening the door just enough so she could talk without exposing me. After only a second, she stepped aside so Keith could enter.

twenty-four

At first no one said anything after Mom closed the door. Keith stood with his hands jammed in his pockets. I could tell that he'd been crying, too. Mom touched his shoulder and sat back down on the bed. "Miranda told me, Keith."

He turned to Mom. "I didn't mean for this to happen."

"I know you didn't."

He looked at me. "Miranda—"

I got off the bed and went to him, putting a finger through one of his belt loops. "I'm sorry that I ran out on you."

He glanced over at Mom, but kissed me and put his hand against my cheek anyway. "It almost killed me when you did."

Mom stood up. "I'm going to let you have some privacy to work this out. Are you going to be able to do that?"

I nodded, even though I wasn't sure that we would be able to agree.

Mom took a deep breath. "I'll support whatever decision you make as long as you make it together." She left the room and closed the door behind her.

"I don't know why I told her that, because I don't know how to solve this," I told Keith, sinking down on one of the star-shaped rugs and leaning up against the bed with my arms folded behind my head.

He sat next to me. "Me neither. I just don't want this to tear us apart."

"That's one thing we agree on." We sat on the floor for a long time, our hands almost touching. staring up at the castle I'd painted on the walls. Finally I said, "Sometimes I wonder if abortion is the right choice, but every time I try to imagine anything else I just end up crying."

Keith took a breath and said, "I guess it's not so much that I want a baby. I want a future. I want to go to college and I want to play ball and I want to write songs and see if anyone wants to listen to me sing them, but more than anything I want to be with you. Part of me thinks that if we choose abortion, we'll be destroying our chances of a future together."

"I don't know if that's true though, Keith. Our relationship isn't going to be like it was, but does that mean it has to be over?"

"I guess part of me thinks if you don't want my baby, maybe you don't want me either." He didn't look at me when he said those words.

I remembered Carly saying almost the same thing about Danny. I put my hand on his leg. "No, that's not why at all. I love you so much."

"Then why can't we—"

I shook my head, interrupting the argument before it started again. "Look, I know you're right about a lot of things, Keith. Our parents would be supportive. And I could probably survive school. No one would be able to say anything worse about me at this point. But there's more to it than that."

"Like what?" Keith asked, his arms folded across his chest even though I'd kept my hand on his thigh.

Instantly my eyes started to tear up, and I squeezed them shut.

Keith put one finger on my hand. "Try and tell me, Miranda. I need to understand."

I wiped the sleeve of my sweater across my eyes. "At night I hold my hands over my stomach for hours, trying to figure out how I can make a decision so no one gets hurt. If I do it your way, I'm going to give up my future. Maybe that's what I deserve for being irresponsible. What kind of life is that though? For you? For a baby? For me?"

"It doesn't have to be all bad though."

I looked at him. Really looked at him. His eyes were steady on mine and I could see that he believed what he was saying.

"Maybe. Maybe you're right, Keith. But you know who you are and what you want. You don't lie to yourself or hurt people like I do."

"You're so hard on yourself."

"No. I'm not hard enough. I've got so much to learn. I'm afraid having a baby now would absorb me just when I'm starting to figure out a few things in my life. I don't want to lose myself again."

Keith intertwined his hand with mine and brought my fingers to his lips. I wiped wetness from my face with my other hand.

"That's probably selfish, isn't?"

He shook his head. "I thought you were being selfish, but I guess I really didn't know you'd thought about it so much or how much it was hurting you. I was being selfish, too, thinking a baby would ensure our future together. Forever."

We sat there for a long time, leaning against my bed, holding hands. Finally Keith said, "I understand why abortion is what you want, but how can you be sure that you won't be sorry later?"

"I guess I'll never be sure. But don't you think that there would be 'what-if's' no matter what?"

"Yeah, probably." We were both silent for a long time and then Keith took a deep breath. "I won't go back to that clinic. I need to be with you. If we can find a place that will let me hold your hand and make sure you're safe and okay, I'll agree to an abortion. But I want you to know that part of me will always be sad about our choice."

I nodded, feeling like I needed to thank him for listening to me and understanding. But he took me into his arms before the words could form. "You don't need to say anything, Miranda. I know, okay?"

Closing my eyes, I held on to him, too, tighter than I ever had before.

epilogue

I've just finished my first year at the Denver Art Institute. Mom and Dad didn't jump out of the pantry yelling, "Happy Birthday!" when I turned nineteen last week. Instead, they left nineteen little gift-wrapped packages on the countertop where I eat my morning yogurt. Dad peeked from around his newspaper when I opened the first present—a tube of acrylic paint. "We thought you might need some art supplies for the fall."

Mom sipped her coffee and slid me a card, but didn't let go until I met her eyes. "I'll always be a little disappointed that you aren't at the university with me, especially when I meet Tasha and Mack for lunch and you aren't with us. But I can see that art school was a good choice for you."

I smiled, "Thanks, Mom."

Dad put down the sports section. "You know, Miranda. I'm working on a project right now that needs some custom painting. It would be a great summer job for you."

I sort of rolled my eyes, and Mom laughed. Dad's trying to recruit me into his business by saying that he'd love to add decorative painting to his company's services. I haven't given him an answer on that yet. There's plenty of time to figure out how I'm going to spend my life.

I'm only certain about one thing for sure, and that's Keith. He decided to go to college in Fort Collins, not because his parents wanted him to go, but because he knows that one day the ranch will be his. A few agriculture classes might help him make better choices in the future. He still plays his guitar on Pearl Street and buys me ice cream with the donations. For my birthday, he took me to

Six Flags again, but this time we let Ali and one of her friends tag along. Driving there we passed a giant billboard with a human baby floating upside down in a tight ball under an anti-abortion slogan. The image loomed up in the window for an instant, then was gone, but Keith looked at me and our hands met.

The image on the billboard stayed in my mind even with the blur of colors on the roller coasters and ferris wheel. Some people might say that's my conscience or my guilt. And I won't deny that getting on that table that day under the white lights changed my life forever. Do I regret my choice? I've thought about that a lot, and I've decided that kind of thinking is about as helpful as chasing castles in the sky.

"What are you thinking about?" Keith asked me later when Ali finally agreed to a couple of hours in the water park. I was spreading suntan lotion on his back and my hand had stopped over his tattoo. I was remembering the first time I'd seen it and how I'd thought it was so sexy. But I can see deeper now. Harmony is Keith. It's his life with music and the way he cares for animals, land, people, and the way he touches me.

Tracing the first Chinese character with my finger, I answered, "I guess I'm thinking that this should be on a billboard."

He twisted around to look at me. "No one would know what it meant."

I shrugged and said, "Yeah, but we would."

And he gave me one of those smiles that will always take my breath away.

the end

acknowledgements

Thanks to all the women who shared the journey—the books, the stories, the songs, the chocolate, the chai, the wine on the stoop in the moonlight. Special gratitude to Pam for turning off the phone; Vera and Portia for never letting me starve; Tracy for understanding secrets; Susan for reading first, Barb for divas; Lora for always being home; Maria for November 20th; Kathy for believing in me; and Mom and Dad for everything always.

Most of all, thanks to the amazing women and men at Hollins University—Amanda, Jeanne, Elizabeth, J.D., Sue, Lisa, Chip, Chip, Ann, Han, Beverly, Shama, Zeta, Nancy, Robin, Durinda, Carter, Betsy, Bethany, and Tyler. And of course, my greatest thanks to Julie Pfeiffer for astonding support and Karen Sulken-Adams for gentle guidance and encouragement every step of the way.

about the author

Michelle Taylor has lived in Colorado most of her thirty-something years. She likes chai tea, homemade pesto, faded jeans, and acoustic guitars. Currently she drives a purple mini-van but dreams of a vintage Mustang with a white leather interior. Love stories come easily for Michelle because she's never forgotten the magic of first kisses and slow dances. When she grows up, she'd like a job naming lipstick and nail polish colors.